Quilt Complex

A Southern Quilting Mystery, Volume 19

Elizabeth Craig

Published by Elizabeth Craig, 2023.

This is a work of fiction. Similarities to real people, places, or events are entirely coincidental.

QUILT COMPLEX

First edition. September 26, 2023.

Written by Elizabeth Craig.

Chapter One

A s soon as she took that last bite of sausage and egg breakfast casserole, Beatrice let out a satisfied sigh. Then a yawn. She said ruefully to her friend and neighbor Meadow, "I can't believe I ate an entire plate of food. I'd already had breakfast before I even came over here."

Meadow looked skeptical of that. "A *real* breakfast? Or one of those so-called breakfasts?"

Meadow staunchly believed that breakfast was the biggest meal of the day. She could feed an army with what she cooked for herself and Ramsay every morning. Blueberry muffins, fluffy pancakes, egg and tomato scrambles, and buttery grits were frequent staples on her table.

"A perfectly acceptable breakfast of cereal and a banana," said Beatrice, just a touch defensively.

Meadow snorted. "That's not enough to feed a mouse. Now you've had a big meal and are equipped to take on your day."

Beatrice yawned again. "I'm equipped to take on a nap, you mean. I feel like going home and crawling back into my bed."

Meadow's reaction to this was to refill Beatrice's coffee mug. "None of that! You've got to help me make plans for the reception. I'm depending on you."

A tired voice came from behind them. "*I'm* depending on you, Beatrice. So I won't have to be the one the ideas are endlessly bouncing off of."

They turned to smile at Meadow's husband, Ramsay. He was a balding man with kind eyes and a stomach that had seen lots of Meadow's good cooking. As the chief of police in Dappled Hills, he was in uniform and looked ready to head out to the station.

Meadow hopped up out of her chair. "Want a muffin for the road?" She gave Ramsay a peck on the cheek.

He gave her a bemused kiss in return. "A muffin? No, no. I'll be like Beatrice . . . in a food coma."

Beatrice chuckled. "Do I look that bad?"

"Not bad at all. Just not particularly alert," said Ramsay. "Which, for police chiefs, is not necessarily a great state to be in at work."

He grabbed a couple of books from the counter, along with a small notebook and a pen, and then waved goodbye and hurried off, presumably before more wedding talk commenced.

Beatrice couldn't blame him. Wedding planning wasn't exactly her forte. She'd planned and executed tons of fundraiser dinners when she'd been an art museum curator, but a wedding was an entirely different kettle of fish. She considered reminding Meadow of this, but Meadow was already launching into her planning.

"So, tell me what you think of this. I'm thinking about candles in mason jars. Won't that be a pretty touch? Or will it be too much, seeing as how the reception is already in a barn? Should I try to plan something swankier?"

Beatrice shook her head. "Swanky doesn't sound like what Tiggy and Dan are looking for."

Tiggy was a fellow quilter in their quilt guild and the aunt of their good friends Savannah and Georgia. Dan was the local handyman and Tiggy's late-in-life romance. They'd shyly accepted Meadow's offer to host their wedding reception at the renovated barn where she and Ramsay lived.

"The problem with mason jars and candles," said Beatrice, "is the fact it's a liability with Boris around."

Boris, Meadow's huge, sweet, but oafish dog, gazed lovingly at Beatrice and at the scraps of food on her plate and grinned at her in agreement.

Meadow beamed at Boris. "He's been so very good lately! I've only caught him eating food off the counters twice in the last week."

Cammie, Meadow's tiny dog, gave Boris a disapproving look. Boris turned his doggy grin on Cammie, tongue lolling out.

Beatrice thought of her extremely well-behaved corgi back at her house. Noo-noo wouldn't dream of trying to grab food off the counters. Naturally, she was extremely short, but even if she had long legs, she wouldn't do it. There was such a thing as manners and Noo-noo understood that very well.

"I think mason jar candles might be a fire risk around Boris," said Beatrice, shaking her head. "And I have the feeling Ramsay will think the same thing."

Meadow nodded slowly. "I suppose you're right. Ramsay can be such a party pooper. But we wouldn't want to ruin the wedding reception with a fire."

"Or your home," said Beatrice wryly.

"No. But that last time I kept Boris in the guest bedroom with a Kong worked out really well. Perhaps I should do that again. He wasn't destructive at all in there."

Beatrice said, "In that case, I think the candle-filled mason jars will work out beautifully. But I remember Dan and Tiggy saying they wanted everything kept very simple. I wouldn't go overboard with the planning."

Meadow waved her hand dismissively. "They're only saying that because they don't want me to go to any trouble. They're both very sweet. But you know I live for this sort of thing. I do love to give a big party." She sighed. "And Ramsay and I had a very sweet wedding, but it wasn't anything much to plan. I loved helping with Ash and Piper's wedding. And yours! Now we have Tiggy and Dan's. Anyway, the point is that they hate the idea of me putting in a lot of time. But it's my pleasure."

Beatrice shook her head uneasily. "I'm not so sure. Sometimes people say exactly what they mean. Plus, they wouldn't want you to go to much expense. I believe they mentioned being on a budget."

"Precisely why I'm doing the catering for them! I'll cook and they only have to pay me for the groceries. The barn is free for them to use. I have a million mason jars left over from all my canning activities. We're running completely to budget. My only wish is that it wasn't such a *rushed* affair. If I had more time to plan it, I could come up with something spectacular."

Beatrice had the feeling that Tiggy and Dan had made it rushed for that very reason. They didn't want something spectacular. With less time for Meadow to plan, they'd end up with the simple, small, wedding they were looking for. Plus, there was another reason, too.

"Another reason to keep things simple is because Dan is about to have the surgery for his Atrial Fibrillation. I understand it can be a little tricky. They wanted to tie the knot before he had his procedure."

Meadow nodded sadly. "You're right. I shouldn't complain. Poor Dan. I hope they're able to get his heart back to working properly. What's the procedure called again?"

"Ablation. I'm sure he'll be fine. He's supposedly got a wonderful cardiologist helping him out."

"Good. I've truly been thinking about Dan a lot. The whole wedding thing has just gotten me sidetracked lately. Maybe I need to bring some food over to him. Or to Tiggy. Or both of them." Meadow now looked as though she was doubling down with her determination to be helpful.

Beatrice said, "Well, it might not be a terrible idea to bring something to Dan. You know what a health nut Tiggy is. She's likely been keeping him on a diet of sprouts and greens. He's probably on a special diet, though, so maybe you could keep in the guidelines for that."

"I *can* cook extremely healthy things. And still make them taste good."

"I know you can," said Beatrice. "At any rate, you'll do a far better job than poor Tiggy. She means well, though."

Meadow looked thoughtful. "Of course, we're going to see Tiggy at the Patchwork Cottage in just a few hours. I can ask her then about Dan's diet." She clapped her hands together, startling little Cammie, who glared at her. Boris just lolled his tongue out, grinning at his mother. "I nearly forgot about our class this morning! Heavens. I was just going to spend the rest of the day looking at wedding websites and trolling for ideas."

"Are the Cut-Ups going to be at the class? Or is it just supposed to be for the Village Quilters?"

Meadow said, "Posy opened it up to everybody, but we're going to have some Village Quilters business to attend to after the class. Nothing much, though, because we don't want to bore the Cut-Ups."

Beatrice stood up and put her plate into Meadow's dishwasher. Boris gave her a reproachful look for not handing it over to him to clean up. "I should be getting along. Thanks so much for the breakfast."

"Thanks for coming over and being a sounding board for me," said Meadow. "See you in a few hours."

Later that morning, Beatrice parked behind the Patchwork Cottage quilt shop and headed into the building. She always loved being there. Posy had music from local musicians playing in the background, sunbeams coming through every window, and a comfortable sitting area with a sweet shop kitty to cuddle with.

Posy's programs were in the back room of the shop, which was more of a bare bones area. Posy had decorated a bit for the class, though, with quilts hanging everywhere and a table full of snacks. From the number of tables and chairs she'd set out, it looked as if she was expecting high attendance.

Posy smiled at Beatrice as she came in. "So glad you could make it," she said, giving her a hug. "I was excited that I could schedule our speaker today. It sounded like she gets pretty booked up."

"I wouldn't miss it," said Beatrice. "I love the idea of mixed media for quilting."

Posy beamed at her. "It's the art curator in you."

"Right. It's also something completely different. I can't wait to hear what she has to say about it. I brought my notebook so I could take a bunch of notes."

Posy said, "Oh, the price of the program also covers a video of her going through it step-by-step. That way, you can watch it again at home when you have all your materials assembled."

"That beats taking notes any day."

One of the Cut-Ups came over and pulled Posy away to ask her advice about a project she was working on. Beatrice walked over to the food table to sample some goodies that Posy had prepared.

Miss Sissy, always ravenous, had been at the table for a while and was now carefully balancing a crustless pimento cheese sandwich on top of a very full plate.

"How are you, Miss Sissy?" asked Beatrice politely.

Miss Sissy snarled a reply. She always did seem fairly unapproachable when she was getting ready to eat. She looked wilder than usual, wearing a polka-dot dress with the hem falling out. To continue the unkempt theme, her iron-gray hair was coming out of her very loose bun. She had a fierce, combative look in her eyes, as if convinced one of the other ladies would steal food from her plate.

"How are you?" asked a voice behind Beatrice.

She turned to give her friend Georgia a hug. Georgia was smiling at her and looked relaxed.

"Doing well! How are you? Are you getting excited about the wedding?"

Georgia nodded. "It seems like everything is coming into place. I was so excited when Wyatt was available to officiate. And having the chapel available at the last minute was also a stroke of luck."

Beatrice took a quick look around to make sure Tiggy wasn't anywhere close. Oddly, she didn't see her. Then, in a low voice, she asked, "Any luck on the wedding dress front?"

The last Beatrice had heard, Tiggy, an enthusiastic but terrible seamstress, had told everyone she was planning on making her own wedding dress. Judging by the horrid concoctions Tiggy had crafted in the past, Beatrice thought this was a very bad idea.

Georgia nodded, chuckling. "Yes, thank heavens. I convinced Tiggy that there wasn't enough time for her to create her own dress, since the wedding is pretty last-minute. I also threw in the fact that she should be pampering herself and not worrying about working hard before the wedding. We've done a little shopping, but everything we've seen has been pretty expensive."

"I bet."

Georgia continued, "We're going on a little shopping trip to Lenoir soon. There's supposed to be a bridal outlet there, and I bet we'll be able to find something pretty and simple for her."

"She couldn't make it to the class today?" asked Beatrice.

Georgia shook her head. "She said she had a couple of errands to run. They might even be errands for Dan. Tiggy's been trying, pretty unsuccessfully, to keep Dan quiet until his procedure."

"Did the doctor want him to take it easy?" asked Beatrice, frowning. "For some reason, I thought AFib patients were supposed to be more active."

Georgia chuckled. "Bingo. Healthy eating, exercise, and good-quality sleep are the things the doctor prescribed. But Tiggy's got her own way of looking after Dan."

"Well, I'm sure she's at least got his healthy eating covered," said Beatrice dryly. Tiggy was quite fond of poorly cooked greens and Brussels sprouts the last she heard. Savannah had been hugely relieved when Tiggy moved out of her place and stopped trying to cook for her.

"You've got that right," said Georgia. "Fortunately, Dan doesn't seem to be that much into food, so he doesn't mind. But the lack of activity is about to drive him up a wall."

"Tiggy will let him work, though, won't she? I know he's in demand."

Dan was one of those men who could do just about anything. For a while, he'd fallen out of favor locally, considered a suspect in a Dappled Hills murder. But once his name was cleared, he was as busy as ever. Unless Tiggy had put a wrench into the works, that was.

Georgia said, "Fortunately, Tiggy has come around to see that income flow is a good thing. But as soon as Dan is done painting a house or repairing an HVAC system, she's got him putting his feet up while she clucks around him like a mama bird."

"It sounds like she'll make sure he recovers from his procedure in record time, considering she's hovering so much!"

Georgia shrugged. "The way the doctors made it sound, Dan will be able to return to work after just a couple of days following the ablation. Whether Tiggy will allow that to happen remains to be seen, of course."

"Got it. How are the rest of the wedding plans going? Meadow was talking about food and candles and other details this morning." Beatrice paused. "How about the bridesmaids' dresses for you and Savannah?"

Georgia grinned. "Fear not. She's not making those, either."

"Well, I know that's a relief," said Beatrice. "It's nice not to have to stress about that."

Still chatting, they filled their plates with food and headed over to the long tables holding sewing machines. A few minutes later, Posy started the meeting.

Chapter Two

The woman giving the program had clearly given a lot of workshops before. She was confident, her voice carried well to even the hardest hearing ears. Plus, she definitely knew her topic. She explained that the mixed media quilting was like another form of storytelling. You could take family keepsakes or relics and turn them into art. After machine quilting a base, the quilter could explore different ways of attaching the objects to the fabric, including pin weaving, grommets, and brads. After the speaker was finished, everyone gave her a round of applause.

The regular guild meeting followed, although it was shortened. Meadow spoke up for a few minutes about how she'd managed to organize her fabric stash. "At first, I was tearing my hair out over this stuff. Fabric everywhere, and it was all different sizes. I tried to sort them by size, but it was way too much work. I didn't have the patience for it. I decided to make two different sizes. Everything would either be cut into five-inch squares or two and a half inch strips. Now it's all a lot easier for me to know what I've got and actually *use* it. Sometimes I feel like all I do is buy fabric, and I have so much of it at home."

This earned Meadow a round of applause, and she beamed at everyone and took a mock curtsy.

Posy made an announcement, reminding everyone to have sewing machine repairmen to check their machines for tension from time to time to make sure it wasn't set too high or too low. She also encouraged the members to donate any quilting books they'd already read to the guild library. "And if you could, write a tiny review of the book. That way, we can put it in our newsletter and other members will get a good idea whether it might help them out or not."

The meeting broke up and everyone started visiting with each other. Piper, Beatrice's daughter, had come in a few minutes late and gave her mom a belated hug when the meeting wrapped up. She had Will with her and the little boy had sat quietly on the floor through the program, courtesy of a couple of toy trucks she'd brought with her.

Meadow, Piper's mother-in-law, hurried over as soon as she spotted her.

"How's the baby?" she asked breathlessly. "He was so good during the class that I couldn't believe it."

Piper chuckled. "He wouldn't thank you for calling him a baby. He's convinced he's a big boy."

"And right he is!" said Meadow. "I have a tough time wrapping my head around that fact, I guess."

"He's doing great," said Piper. "I got out of the house a little late, but at least I managed to get over here. I love multimedia quilts. I'll have to give it a try once I have more time."

Meadow quickly said, "If you need more time, let me know!
I'll babysit. This is the first time I've laid eyes on Will since I
started doing all the wedding planning."

"I can babysit too," said Beatrice, not wanting to get edged
out by Meadow, who could be aggressive when it came to getting time with Will.

Miss Sissy, finished with food for at least the time being,
headed over to see Will. The little boy loved the old woman, and
she played with him like she was a child herself. Sure enough,
she plucked him right from Piper's arms and they trotted over to
see Maisie, the shop cat. Maisie was wearing a particularly fetching outfit that Georgia had made: a shirt that said Patchwork
Paws.

More quilters had come over to speak with Piper and Meadow and Beatrice slipped away for another sugar cookie. She'd
have to ask Posy how hers were so moist. However, Beatrice suspected that even if she knew the secret behind Posy's cookies,
she wouldn't be able to replicate them.

She was sitting quietly at the table when she heard a couple
of the Cut-Ups talking with each other. It wasn't that Beatrice
was *trying* to eavesdrop. It was simply that they were speaking
very loudly over the general chatty din of the room.

"What do you think is going to happen with Thea?" asked
a thin woman with piercing eyes. Beatrice knew some of the
women in the Cut-Ups guild, but these women were two that
she recognized but hadn't formally met.

The other woman with black hair and rather a lot of makeup
said, "Who knows? Mona was saying Thea simply couldn't be

trusted anymore. That when that bond of trust is broken, that things can't go back to the way they were before."

The woman with the piercing eyes said, "That seems kind of harsh, doesn't it? It wasn't *that* big of a deal."

"It was," said the woman with the makeup. "Of course it was. I don't have a problem keeping it between ourselves, but there still have to be consequences for her actions."

"Let's think about it," said the other woman. "We're really all she has, don't you think? She's divorced and works all the time. I'd hate for her to lose the one outlet she has."

They were joined by a lively group of the other Cut-Ups, and the private conversation ended. Although Beatrice was still wondering about it later.

Georgia, seeing Beatrice was sitting alone, sat down beside her. "What are your plans for the rest of the day?" asked Beatrice.

"I think I might stick my head in next door at the boutique. Just to see what kinds of dresses they have in there," said Georgia. She grimaced. "Although I have the feeling they're going to be pricy ones."

"You mean for Tiggy?" asked Beatrice, raising her eyebrows in surprise. "I wasn't aware they sold wedding dresses in there."

"Oh, I don't think they do. But they might have something appropriate. Tiggy said she'd consider non-traditional wedding dresses, too . . . maybe a cream-colored suit or something. She thought, as an older bride, it might be more appropriate. Anyway, I figured before we made the trek to Lenoir, I might as well check to make sure there isn't something in Dappled Hills we could use."

"Good point," said Beatrice. She paused. "I've never been in there for the same reason—I think it's probably pricy. Mind if I pop in there with you?"

"Sure. I could actually really use a second opinion. Plus, I always get very awkward when I enter a small shop and don't buy anything. I always feel I should get *something* or else it looks like I don't like the merchandise." Georgia shrugged and laughed. "You'd think I was still a kid."

"No, I totally get that. But I'm not that way at all, so I can extricate you from the shop with no trouble. If there's nothing in there that suits us, we can simply politely leave."

Georgia looked relieved. "That would be amazing. Thanks, Beatrice."

They helped Posy pick up trash and put some of the folding chairs away. Beatrice gave Piper and Will a hug goodbye and set out with Georgia for the boutique next door. The store was called Mountain Chic and, judging from the elegant outfits in the window, seemed aptly named.

Georgia said under her breath, "I have the feeling this is going to be a dead end."

"Well, let's just check and see. Like you said, it would be nice to be able to find something for Tiggy here instead of having to drive to another town for a shopping trip."

They walked into the cool interior of the shop, a bell on the door announcing their arrival.

Georgia said quietly, "It's lucky that no one's here to greet us. Maybe we can give the place a quick glance and head back out." She glanced around. "This place *looks* expensive."

Beatrice could see what she meant. The walls were adorned with textured, reclaimed wood. There were large floor-to-ceiling windows with a view of one of the mountain peaks. The lighting was soft and ambient and flattering to shoppers. There was a shimmering chandelier hanging gracefully from the wooden ceiling, sending a soft glow over the display tables and racks of clothing. The whole atmosphere was one of sophistication and opulence.

They started looking through the merchandise. Although the boutique wasn't large, it seemed to stock quite a variety of luxury items. Beatrice recognized the names on a couple of designer labels. There was everything from soft cashmere sweaters, silk blouses, and finely tailored dresses. There was a section of the store that seemed to be for special occasions, and many of the dresses appeared to be mother-of-the-bride and mother-of-the-groom dresses. Georgia looked at one of the price tags and gave Beatrice a look. Beatrice said, "Let's keep looking. Maybe there's a clearance section."

"You're right. That's a great idea."

"If they have one, it's probably at the back of the store."

Beatrice and Georgia crossed to the back of the store. Sure enough, there seemed to be a section with marked-down clothing. It was a mishmash, though, of both casual and dressy and of various sizes. The markdowns didn't seem to be that significant to Beatrice's untrained eye. At any rate, the clothing was a lot more than she'd want to spend.

Georgia pulled out a couple of things and studied them. "I don't know. What do you think? This should be Tiggy's size."

Beatrice cocked her head to one side. "I'm not sure about the glittery stuff on the shoulders. It doesn't seem like something Tiggy would wear."

Georgia peaked at the price tag and gasped. "Even if she would, she couldn't handle the price tag. That barely seems reduced. Well, I guess it was worth a try. Let's slip out before we get noticed."

In Georgia's eagerness to avoid any awkwardness with the store owner, she hurried toward the door. But Beatrice's gaze had been caught by something else.

"Beatrice?" asked Georgia from the front of the store.

Beatrice let out a wordless breath, her eyes fixed on a woman's lifeless body on the floor. She'd been strangled with a scarf.

Chapter Three

Georgia moved hesitantly forward, seeing Beatrice's face. "Oh no," she gasped, covering her mouth with one hand.

Beatrice was pulling her phone out of the pocket of her black slacks. "Do you know who she is?"

Georgia shook her head. "Maybe the owner? Or at least someone who worked here." She turned away, unable to look at the woman and her staring eyes any longer. The woman was stylish-looking, and the cream-colored suit was likely from the boutique's own collection. She wore delicate gold jewelry.

With shaking fingers, Beatrice dialed Ramsay's number.

He immediately answered. "I hope you're not asking for advice on Tiggy and Dan's wedding," Ramsay said in a joking tone.

"I wish that's what I was calling about. Ramsay, there's a dead body at the boutique downtown. I'm with Georgia, and she and I aren't sure who it is."

There was a momentary pause before Ramsay's grim voice said, "I'll be right there."

Considering the police station was a few doors down, he really was right there. By that time, Georgia and Beatrice had carefully removed themselves from the shop, standing near the front door of Mountain Chic.

"She's in the back corner," said Beatrice as Ramsay approached them.

He gave her a curt nod, put disposable booties over his shoes, and then hurried into the shop.

"How awful," said Georgia in a shaky whisper.

A few minutes later, Ramsay came back out. He'd brought a roll of police tape with him, and he carefully strung it up.

"The state police are on their way over," he said. "How about if the two of you tell me what happened to Mona Peters?"

"That's her name?" whispered Georgia. "Was she the one who owned the shop?"

Ramsay nodded. "She and I had spoken a few times."

Beatrice and Georgia looked at each other, and Georgia motioned for Beatrice to go ahead. Beatrice said, "Unfortunately, we don't know much about what actually happened to Mona. Georgia and I were over with the rest of the guild at the Patchwork Cottage for a program. Georgia mentioned she wanted to stick her head in the boutique and see if she could find an appropriate wedding dress for Tiggy."

Ramsay nodded. "So you went in right after the program."

"Right. At first we didn't see her. Mona was tucked into the back of the store. Georgia and I were back there, looking through the sale section. We didn't see anything that looked right for Tiggy, so Georgia headed for the door. I glanced around and saw Mona." Beatrice swallowed, her mouth suddenly feeling dry.

Ramsay nodded. "And no one else was in the store?"

They both shook their heads. "No one," said Georgia.

"Did you see anyone leaving the store when you were coming in?"

They shook their heads again.

"Okay," said Ramsay. "Thanks for filling me in."

A deputy joined Ramsay, and he moved away from them to speak with him.

There was a voice behind Beatrice and Georgia. "What's going on?"

They turned around to see a big, blustering man with a florid face. He gestured to the crime scene tape on the boutique door. "Obviously, *something* is going on. I own the restaurant next door. Josh Copeland."

Beatrice said quietly, "The shop owner has died."

Josh's eyes grew wide, and he had a faint, incredulous smile on his face. "Mona Peters is dead?"

Ramsay turned to glance briefly at him before turning back around to continue giving the deputy instructions. Beatrice wasn't surprised that he turned. Josh sounded rather delighted by the fact that Mona was no longer alive.

Maybe Josh realized appearances might be important, because he suddenly sobered. "That's quite a surprise. What happened? Did she have a heart attack? Mona was always so tightly wound up about everything. I knew that stress level couldn't be good for her health."

Ramsay joined them again. "Hi there, Josh. No, it wasn't a heart attack. It's a suspicious death."

Josh's eyes grew wide again. "Murder? Mona was murdered?"

Ramsay nodded. "It sure looks that way."

"What happened?"

Ramsay said, "I can't disclose any of the details." He took out his notebook. "Since your restaurant is right next door, maybe you can help me out. Where were you this morning?"

"Me? I was at the restaurant, as usual. I checked in a food delivery and was helping the staff get ready for the lunch rush." Josh's tone was a bit defensive. He took a small step backward, as if wanting to escape back to the safety of his restaurant.

Ramsay made a careful note of this. "Did you happen to notice anything unusual this morning? Was there anybody lurking around? Did you notice any of the customers coming into or out of the shop?"

Josh pointed at Beatrice and Georgia. "Well, these two ladies."

Ramsay nodded. "They were in a quilting program all morning, so they're accounted for. Did you notice anyone else?"

Josh shook his head, still looking a bit defensive. "No. I was busy, as I mentioned. I didn't have the time or interest in monitoring what was going on next door. As far as I was concerned, it was an ordinary Saturday, until now."

Ramsay made a couple of notes. He turned a piercing gaze on Josh. "Now, you must know I have to bring up the calls the station has received in the past." He glanced at Beatrice and Georgia. "Perhaps you'd like to speak with me privately about those."

Josh paled a little before his face returned to its normal, reddish hue. "I don't have anything to hide."

"A neighboring business recently called the station to say you and Mona were having a huge argument over parking spaces." Ramsay tapped his pen on the notepad.

Josh shrugged. "That didn't mean anything at all. Mona and I are two people who care passionately about our businesses. I want what's best for my restaurant and she wanted the same for her boutique. As you know, there isn't enough parking downtown. Sometimes Mona's customers parked where they weren't supposed to. I *need* those spots for the restaurant. So yes, occasionally we squabbled over petty stuff like that. But it wasn't a big deal. If nothing else, it showed we had a lot in common—we cared about our businesses."

Ramsay made a few notes. "Okay. There was another call recently, too. Mona called the station because she said the restaurant's music was too loud."

Josh snorted. "Right. That was an example of Mona being completely unreasonable. She was complaining about the music we pipe outdoors for the patio tables that line the street. It's completely innocuous and meant to be background noise. It's not as if we were playing hard rock. She was off-base, but again, it's just an example of the fact that she cared about making a perfect experience for her customers. As you may have heard, the first thing I thought of when I was told Mona had died was that she must have had a heart attack. She was very Type-A."

"Got it. Since you knew Mona pretty well, why don't you give me your impressions of her." He gave Josh a smile, but Ramsay's eyes were guarded.

Josh looked at Ramsay. "Did you know Mona?"

Ramsay nodded. "We were acquainted, yes."

"What did *you* make of her?"

Ramsay quirked an eyebrow. "I'm the one doing the questioning right now."

Josh flushed. "Well, let's say that Mona could be a pain to deal with, to be perfectly honest. She was the kind of person who could fly off the handle at a moment's notice. You'd never seen it coming. The littlest thing could set her off. Whenever she had something to complain about, she'd go right in with all guns blazing. There would be no small talk. There was no subtlety there at all. Mona was very direct. She'd get furious over tiny things and would yell at the top of her lungs. I always felt sorry for her husband." He put his hand over his mouth. "I wish I hadn't said that. He's going to have to find out that he lost his wife this morning."

"Do you know her husband?" asked Ramsay.

"I wouldn't say I know Dillon well, but he was over at the shop sometimes. He'll grab a bite to eat over at the restaurant sometimes, too. Seems like a nice guy. He's got to be pretty laid back to be able to balance out Mona."

Ramsay said, "Do you have any ideas about who might have done this? Did Mona ever mention having any trouble with anybody? Did you pick up on anything that seemed unusual?"

Josh thought about this for a minute. "Well, I don't know if it was anything *unusual*, but I did notice that young woman who used to work at the boutique. I can't remember her name."

"She doesn't work at Mountain Chic anymore?"

"Nope. Mona fired her. Mona had a way of running through staff. It was crazy to me. There aren't that many people to hire in this town. You have to treat your staff like they're gold because you might not be able to find a replacement when they're gone. But Mona was pretty rough on them."

Ramsay asked, "Rough on them? How?"

Josh shrugged. "This is all hearsay from folks Mona has run off through the years. Basically, Mona was expecting too much. Too many hours, too much perfection. She wanted the staff to look a particular way; they always had to be perfectly groomed and wearing swanky clothes. Clothes from the boutique. Now, how could those kids who worked there afford to buy those clothes? Have you seen those price tags?"

The question was directed at Beatrice and Georgia and they both nodded. Ramsay frowned. "How *did* they afford those clothes, then?"

"Mona gave them a nominal discount, but it wasn't much. I guess the poor kids would wear the same thing a few times a week. But it wasn't just her expectations for how she wanted her staff to look. The store and the merchandise had to be perfect in every way. The displays had to be just so. The clothes had to be folded a particular way. She had them cleaning the windows, too. It seemed like a lot."

Ramsay said, "You know a lot about the day-to-day running of the boutique."

"Like I said, I've talked to the girls Mona fired over the years. Some of them came right next door to ask me for work, and I was always delighted to help them out. If nothing else, Mona had sure trained them to be great employees. They were all conscientious kids and had a real eye for detail. The young woman Mona fired most recently asked me for a job, too. She also had a huge list of complaints about Mona and how she treated her."

"Did you hire her at your restaurant?" asked Ramsay.

Josh shook his head. "No. This time, I didn't hire one of Mona's ex-employees. For one thing, we didn't have any openings for a server. For another, the way she was talking about the boutique made me think she might be one of those workers who complains all the time. That's not great for a positive work environment."

Ramsay jotted down some notes. "And this young woman. How did she seem?"

"Well, agitated about losing her job, and angry when she mentioned Mona. Aside from that, I'd say she seemed pretty desperate. Like she *needed* a job. There was talk about rent and whatnot. Who knows—maybe she murdered Mona out of revenge for putting her in that situation."

"Seems like an unlikely way to get a job back, to murder the owner," said Ramsay. "Do you know why she was fired?"

"No. But it must have been something bad because she didn't want to disclose it."

Ramsay asked for a description of the young woman, which Josh provided. Josh, seeming a bit antsy, said, "Is it okay if I head back to the restaurant? We're in the middle of the lunch rush now."

"Sure. I'll know how to find you if I have more questions."

Chapter Four

Josh left with a look of relief on his face. Ramsay turned to Beatrice and Georgia. "You two are free to head off, too. Sorry that you had to find Mona like that. You doing okay?" He peered closely at them as if he might be able to tell from their faces.

The women nodded at them.

Ramsay said, "Okay, good. You think about getting some self-care this afternoon. Take it easy. That was quite a shock for the both of you. I'll talk to you later if I think of anything else."

They headed toward the parking lot where Beatrice had her car and Georgia had her bike. Georgia said, "What a terrible thing. I can't believe that happened right here in downtown."

Beatrice nodded. "For neither of us to know her, I guess she must have kept to herself."

"Her name is familiar to me, though. I mean, I didn't know her well, obviously, but I feel like I met her or talked to her or heard others talk about her. But I can't remember how. It sounds like she was so caught up in her business, so she might not have gotten out much," said Georgia.

Beatrice nodded. "It sounded like she might have cared a little *too* much about her business, to the extent of running off her staff. If she was a tough person to like, there might be a few suspects." She paused. "I think I'm going to go back to the Patchwork Cottage and chat with Posy for a few minutes about Mona. Since the boutique was so close, Posy might have known her. Do you want to come with me?"

Georgia shook her head. "Ordinarily, I'd love to talk to Posy. But finding Mona shook me up too much. I'm thinking I'd better head home and get a hug from Tony."

Beatrice said, "Let me give you a hug, too. It was a rough end to the morning. Are you sure you're okay to bike home? Do you want me to drive you? Tony could bring you back downtown later to get your bike."

Georgia and her sister biked everywhere. But it didn't seem to Beatrice like a safe mode of transport if someone had a lot on her mind.

Georgia gave her a smile. "Thanks, Beatrice. I promise I'm all right. Riding the bike relaxes me. I think it's going to be a good way to work everything out. I'll see you around soon."

With that, Georgia headed off. Beatrice walked back into the Patchwork Cottage. While there'd likely been a mad rush for supplies after the program ended, the shop was blissfully quiet now, aside from Miss Sissy's snoring emanating from the sitting area.

Posy looked up when the door opened. "Beatrice," she said with a smile. "Thanks so much for coming this morning. And for helping me put the back room to rights again after the program." She paused, looking at Beatrice's grim face searchingly. "Did something happen?"

Beatrice nodded. "Georgia and I went over to the boutique. She wanted to see if there might be a dress that would work as a wedding dress for Tiggy."

Posy brightened. "I heard that Tiggy had been persuaded not to make her own wedding dress."

"Yes, that's definitely a good thing. Anyway, we popped in to look around. We didn't find anything for Tiggy, but we did find the owner. She'd been murdered."

Posy gave a little gasp and put her hands over her mouth. "No!"

Beatrice nodded. "Did you know her well?"

"Mona? No, I wouldn't say I knew her well. I don't shop there, of course, but there were chamber of commerce meetings where we'd go over collective marketing ideas for downtown Dappled Hills."

Beatrice asked, "What did you make of Mona?"

"She always seemed very professional. Mona was always at the meetings on time and was always very stylish—very fashionably dressed. She was sort of a walking advertisement for Mountain Chic. I got along with her fine. But that might be because I have parking behind the store. She and Josh, who owns the restaurant, squabbled all the time. It was mainly over parking spots, but they argued over other things, too. Hearing the two of them argue was pretty stressful, at least for me. The other business owners looked like they were used to it. I guess I was *used* to it, but it still bothered me."

Beatrice said wryly, "Josh didn't exactly look devastated over Mona's death."

"No, I suppose he wouldn't. Gracious. You don't think he had anything to do with it, do you?"

Beatrice said, "I have no idea. It seemed like Ramsay was interested in talking to him, though. He certainly seemed to have a motive. Plus, he could easily have slipped away from the restaurant, murdered Mona, and returned to work as if nothing happened."

Posy nodded slowly. "That's very true." She sighed. "I knew Mona from the shop, too. She was one of the Cut-Ups."

"*Was* she? I didn't realize that. I'm not acquainted with all the members of the guild, but I feel like I'd at least recognize the ones I don't know."

Posy said, "She was, but she didn't attend all the meetings. I don't think she liked participating in the quilt shows or doing any competitions. Oh, that's not really fair of me. As a small business owner, she probably simply didn't have the time to devote to her hobby. I believe she was trying to get back into it, though. She'd bought some fabric and notions from me lately."

"Georgia did mention to me that Mona's name was familiar to her. I'm guessing that's probably why. What did the other members of the Cut-Ups think of Mona? Did they say?"

Posy considered this. "Honestly, I believe there was some sort of falling-out between Mona and some of the guild members. But I don't know anything about it." She paused. "Does Ramsay think that the murderer was somebody who knew Mona? Or do you think he's concerned about the general safety in downtown?"

Posy looked concerned and had a right to be. Beatrice knew that Posy was often alone in the shop. Plus, business would be sure to take a hit if people started considering downtown Dappled Hills to be dangerous. She said, "I'm guessing that Ramsay is probably prioritizing investigating people with a grudge against Mona. It does sound like she could be difficult to deal with. But it wouldn't hurt to lock the door when you're here after the shop closes. I know sometimes you work late."

Posy nodded absently, looking troubled.

Beatrice gave her a hug. "I'm sure everything will work out fine. Ramsay and the state police are on the job. This investigation will all be tied up in no time."

Posy hugged her back. "Thanks, Beatrice."

Beatrice told Posy goodbye and then hopped into the car and headed back home. When she got home, her husband Wyatt was in the front yard, trimming the bushes. He pushed a lock of his silver-streaked hair out of his eyes, grinning at her. Noo-noo, their corgi, was also outside, "helping" Wyatt, mainly by keeping a lookout for squirrels and doves, the two creatures Noo-noo believed had no place in their yard. Beatrice sat down on a small wooden bench that the two of them had recently bought at a craft fair. The yard was shaded by a towering oak and the canopy provided by a couple of red maples. This year, Wyatt and Beatrice had planted wildflowers and the front yard was riotous with color.

"Everything okay?" he asked, quickly picking up on Beatrice's tension as she sat on the bench.

She shook her head. "Everything is fine with me, but it was a very unsettling morning. Georgia and I went into the boutique next door to the Patchwork Cottage to see if we could find a wedding dress for Tiggy. We found the owner, Mona Peters, had been murdered."

"Oh no." Wyatt slowly came over and sat next to her on the bench. He reached out to squeeze her hand. They sat there quietly for a few moments.

"Did you know her at all?" asked Beatrice. "Mona?"

Wyatt frowned, thinking. "I know she was the boutique owner. I've seen her in church from time to time, although she didn't regularly attend. Do you know any details about what happened?"

Beatrice quickly filled him in. "And that's all I know. Georgia was pretty shaken up, which I totally understand. It's the kind of thing that sticks with you."

Wyatt nodded. "I'm sorry you and Georgia had to be the ones to find Mona, but I'm glad you were there with Georgia. I'm sure it helped steady her."

Beatrice's phone started ringing from the pocket of her slacks. "That's probably Piper, if I had to guess."

Sure enough, it was. She was calling in to make sure her mom was okay after Georgia had called to tell her what happened.

"I'm all good, sweetie. But I feel very sorry for Mona."

Piper said, "I know. I can't believe that happened to her. Right there in the middle of Dappled Hills, too. And on a Saturday! That's like the busiest day of the week. And all of us were right next door at the class. Somebody was very brazen."

"Or really depraved. Or desperate. Had you ever met her?"

Piper said, "I did one time. I think it was before you moved here from Atlanta. I was with a friend of mine who was shopping for a special event."

"That makes sense. It does seem like a special event type of place. When Georgia and I were rifling through the racks, it seemed like the prices were super high."

"I guess she was depending on tourists to buy things. Or maybe she had an online store in addition to her physical store. Anyway, when I met her, she was pleasant, but I sort of felt like I wasn't dressed nicely enough to be shopping there. Do you know what I mean? Mona seemed like she was condescending. Or like maybe she thought we couldn't afford to shop there. Which, in my case anyway, was totally true," said Piper with a laugh.

"From everything I've heard so far, it sounds like Mona could have been a tough person to get along with."

"Which means there will be plenty of suspects for Ramsay to question," said Piper ruefully. "I guess there's not going to be a lot of granddad time for Will coming up. He'll have to come over and play with you and Wyatt soon. Which reminds me—church and Sunday lunch tomorrow?"

"Sounds like a plan," said Beatrice.

Piper chuckled. "Do you like how I skillfully invited the family over to eat at your house tomorrow?"

"I'd do the same thing if I were in your shoes! But you know you won't get anything fancy over here. It might be grilled cheese sandwiches with canned tomato soup."

Piper said, "Right now, that sounds amazing. Mainly because it means that *I* won't have to prepare it." She paused. "We could invite Meadow and end up with a real feast."

Beatrice said, "Much as I love Meadow, I don't think losing my personal Will time is going to be worth the luxury of her cooking. You know how much she hogs the baby when she's around."

"I sure do," said Piper wryly. "Okay, we'll leave her out of things this time around. See you tomorrow at the service."

Chapter Five

The rest of Saturday was a lot quieter than the earlier half had been. Wyatt and Noo-noo came in from the yard. Wyatt got cleaned up and then made them both a hot lunch of hot dogs and French fries. He reviewed his sermon for the next day while Beatrice looked for items she could use for her mixed media quilt. Listening to the program at the Patchwork Cottage had inspired her to create a mixed media quilt of her own. She liked the idea of using keepsakes and preserving memories in a new way. She decided to make a quilt that would remind her of her mother. She had a storage box in the closet with her mom's button collection, her favorite apron, and a few other things. Having the items in a quilt as something she saw every day seemed like a better way of remembering her.

The next morning, Beatrice and Wyatt headed to the church early. He was teaching a Sunday school class, and she was attending another one. Piper joined up with Beatrice in the sanctuary before the service started.

"No Ash?" asked Beatrice.

Piper shook her head. "He needed to get a head start grading papers. It goes a lot quicker when Will isn't there. Otherwise, he ends up sitting on the floor and building block towers. This way, Ash can get his work done, Will can play in the church nursery, and you and I can catch up a little."

The service went beautifully, with a lovely solo from one of the best singers in the choir, sunlight streaming through the stained-glass windows, and an earnest and meaningful sermon from Wyatt on love being a verb.

Afterwards, Piper and she picked Will up at the nursery, settled him into his car seat, and Piper drove Beatrice back to her cottage. Beatrice said, "I meant what I said about grilled cheese. I can't seem to wrap my head around cooking these days. I want to eat, but I don't want to prepare it, and I have no creative ideas whatsoever. Or, if I *do* have any creative ideas, they're limited to quilting."

"Grilled cheese is a great comfort food. And I think you could use a little comfort after what happened yesterday. Actually, *I* could use a little comfort. I hate to think you were right in the same vicinity of a killer. What if you had surprised him on his way out of the shop?"

Beatrice said in a light voice, "Oh, I think Georgia and I could have taken him."

They walked into the cottage where Noo-noo greeted Piper and Will ecstatically. Her big brown eyes were filled with joyful surprise, and her entire demeanor stated, "Hey there! No one told me you were coming! This is the best day, ever!"

Will gave a throaty laugh as Noo-noo wiggled next to him. "Good dog!" he said, patting Noo-noo gently.

Piper said, "How about if I give you a break and make the sandwiches for you, Mama?"

Beatrice snorted. "I think I need to give *you* a break. You're the one with a toddler in the house. You should head for the guest room and put your feet up for a while."

"If I put my feet up, the danger is that I'll never get up again," said Piper with a chuckle. "No, grilled cheese sandwiches are easy. I'll get a better break if you play with Will for a while."

"Mission accepted," said Beatrice with relief. She walked over to the coat closet and pulled out the box that had all of Will's toys and books for when he visited.

Will trotted over to join her. "*Poky Puppy*?" he asked.

At this point, Beatrice could recite *The Poky Little Puppy* completely from memory. It had been Piper's Little Golden Book originally and was already in disreputable condition from repeated reading decades ago. But the joy in her grandson's face when she snuggled next to him on the sofa and read the story was worth every bit of it. Will seemed to delight in the fact that the poky puppy got his comeuppance at the end of the book. You can only be poky for so long, after all.

Wyatt came in a few minutes after. "The sandwiches smell great, Piper," he called out. "Can I give you a hand?"

So Wyatt laid the table for them and cut up some finger foods for Will. Beatrice smiled as Wyatt did exactly as he'd seen Piper do on previous occasions and cut grapes and bananas into bits. They all settled at the table, blessed the food, and enjoyed every bite.

"It's a good thing you made enough sandwiches to feed an army," said Beatrice.

"Who knew we were basically going to *be* an army today?" asked Wyatt with a smile. "I guess preaching makes me hungry."

Piper said, "Well, I hoped y'all were as hungry as I was today. But now that we're done, I need to do something active or else I'm going to end up in a food coma."

"Do you need to get back home or can we go to the park?" asked Beatrice. "A little activity sounds good to me, too."

Piper glanced at the clock. "I think Ash would be delighted if we were out of the house for another hour or so. We could walk to the park and let Will play on the playground for a while, if that sounds good."

"Perfect. Want to go with us, Wyatt?" asked Beatrice.

He gave her a wry look. "I'm not going to resist temptation this time. I'm giving into the food coma that Piper mentioned. A nap's going to be in order for me. And for Noo-noo, too."

Noo-noo looked as if she could barely keep her eyes open. But then, she'd been scavenging under Will's chair when he was eating.

So Beatrice and Piper set off with Will to the park. The weather forecasters had claimed there would be showers during the afternoon, but there currently wasn't a cloud in the sky. Will wanted to be a big boy and walk without the umbrella stroller, so Piper held one hand and Beatrice held his other. They stopped from time to time to look at sights along the way. One yard in particular held Will's interest. It was a wildflower garden at a house several doors down from the church. The owners had planted coneflowers, milkweed, Black-Eyed Susans, butterfly weed, and mountain laurel. It was a cacophony of color and butterflies, bumblebees, and hummingbirds were happily enjoying the pollinator garden.

The park was nestled right in the middle of downtown, across from the shops. It had benches scattered throughout, a climbing wall and older child playground, and a playground for small children, too. There were also walking trails that curved through the grounds and connected to the trailhead for a mountain hike. Beatrice spotted a few picnickers at the central open area that served as a gathering place for events and community gatherings. Beatrice would sometimes head over to the park to sit on one of the benches in front of the water feature that had been recently installed there. It was a relaxing place to collect her thoughts.

But today was not going to be a day for relaxation—playtime was in order. Will wanted to swing first, which Beatrice was all in favor of. When he inevitably went to the slides, it was a bit more of an active activity with Beatrice assisting Will at the stairs on the way up and Piper hovering at the bottom of the slide for the way down.

As they walked over to the swings, Piper said quietly, "Isn't that Bibi Norton over there? I didn't realize she had any kids."

"Who?" asked Beatrice.

"She worked for Mona at the boutique. I'm acquainted with her—she's friends with a friend of mine."

Beatrice raised her eyebrows. "Oh, got it. The restaurant owner next door said that Mona had fired her and she'd looked for a job at the restaurant but he didn't have any openings. That's terrible if she has a child to support, too."

Piper waved to Bibi as they approached, and Bibi gave a small wave back. Bibi had a real sense of style, even at the playground. She was wearing expensive looking jeans and a blue and white striped tee shirt. Her blonde hair was pulled back in a headband, creating a deliberately retro look.

"Hi Bibi," said Piper. "This is my mom, Beatrice."

"It's good to meet you," said Beatrice with a smile.

"Likewise," said Bibi with a bob of her head.

Piper put Will in the swing and gave him a push to start him off. "I didn't realize you had any kids. What's your little boy's name? He's very cute."

Bibi blinked and then said, "Oh, he's not mine. I've been taking on some babysitting. I can't even find somebody to be in a relationship with, much less have kids with. Anyway, yeah, I'm babysitting, in case you ever need anybody. I haven't seen you around lately to tell you that I got fired from my job."

Piper did an excellent job of acting as if this was the first time she'd heard anything about this. "I'm so sorry to hear that."

Bibi shrugged. "I know, right? It's not like there are a ton of places to find jobs here, either. I've tried restaurants, the grocery store, and the gas station. Nobody seems to need anyone right now." She absently pushed the boy on the swing. "And that's not the end of my problems. I guess you know Mona was murdered, right? My boss at the boutique?"

Piper nodded. "I'm so sorry about that. I realize she fired you, but it must have been such a shock to hear about it."

Bibi gave a stiff bob of her head. "Yeah. Even worse, it was a shock to realize that the cops thought I might have killed her." She paused, her eyes opening wide. "Hey, your father-in-law is the police chief, right?"

Piper nodded again.

Bibi said, "Do you know anything about what's going on? I mean, did Ramsay have to talk to me mainly because I used to work with Mona? Or am I like a major suspect?"

Then, to Beatrice and Piper's dismay, Bibi burst into tears.

Beatrice took over pushing both boys on the swings while Piper gave Bibi a hug.

After a few moments, Bibi said in a strangled voice, "Oh my gosh. I'm so sorry. I promise I'm not such a crybaby. But lately, I always feel like I'm one step away from boo-hooing."

"Don't be silly. You're under a lot of stress," said Piper. "You've lost your job, you're job hunting, and now this happens? Of course you're going to be upset. That's only natural."

Bibi sniffed and nodded. She rummaged around in the day-pack she wore for a pack of tissues. She said ruefully, "These were supposed to be for the kids, not for me."

Bibi swabbed her nose, then her eyes, then resumed her station at the swings. "Thanks, Beatrice."

Piper took back over swinging Will, and Beatrice stepped back a little. But not far enough so she couldn't hear their conversation.

Piper said slowly, "To answer your question, Ramsay doesn't talk about his cases with me, or Ash, either. But I know, generally, how it all works. The police have to cast a pretty wide net to make sure they speak to everyone who has had contact with the victim. They collect information and then narrow things down. When he spoke to you, it was at the very beginning of the investigation."

Bibi took a deep breath. "Got it. Okay. Well, considering the fact I don't have an alibi and wasn't crazy about Mona to begin with, I'm sure I've put myself closer to the top of the list of suspects." She gave a frustrated shake of her head. "I wish I'd known what had happened. I'd have sounded a lot less suspicious. As it was, I was so shocked to hear about Mona's death that I know I was babbling. I'd been out yesterday morning, running errands before my babysitting gig. I wasn't at home. Even if I *was* at home, I live by myself, so that wouldn't have helped at all."

"I'm sure most people don't have an alibi," said Piper soothingly. "On a beautiful Saturday morning, most folks would have been out of the house."

Bibi brightened at this. "That's probably true. I hope Ramsay realizes that I'm not the kind of person who seeks revenge when things don't work out for me. I mean, who tries to get revenge on someone who fires them? It's not like that would have helped my situation at all. And being a suspect in a murder investigation sure doesn't help me find a job." She gestured to the little boy in the swing, who was looking relaxed and sleepy. "As soon as word gets out that the police have been talking to me in relation to Mona's death, do you think I'll be able to get any babysitting gigs? I'm sure that's going to dry up *real* quick. No one is going to want to entrust their kids to someone who might be a murderer."

"I hope Ramsay will wrap up this investigation quickly," said Piper.

"Me too. Part of me had thought maybe Mona would get over being annoyed with me and give me my old job back. She hadn't hired a replacement for me yet. I was wondering if maybe she wasn't even looking for anybody. That maybe she'd give me a phone call and expect me to grovel." She snorted. "I'd have groveled, for sure. I like eating, and I don't have a lot of savings built up. Besides, Mona wasn't the kind of person who liked to be in the boutique by herself. She was always antsy, always straightening displays or folding and refolding clothes. If I were working, it meant less time she'd have to spend in Mountain Chic. She could do other things. Run errands. Have lunch with her husband or whatnot."

Piper said, "Did Mona lay you off because she needed to cut back on staffing?"

"No, she thought I was asking for too much time off."

But Bibi hesitated before answering and flushed a little. It clearly wasn't the whole story. Beatrice thought that maybe Josh, from the restaurant, had a better idea: that Mona had accused Bibi of some sort of impropriety.

Bibi continued in a rush. "I mean, I respected Mona to a certain degree. She was a strong woman with a great sense of style. She opened and ran her own business, pretty much single-handedly. And the shop was successful, from what I could see. We had good foot traffic, especially when it's high season for tourists. Plus, we had plenty of internet sales. Mona was good with her website and Mountain Chic came up quickly on Google."

Beatrice asked, "Did you enjoy working there?"

Bibi smiled at her. "Most of the time. You know how it is, dealing with the public. But I liked the customers, for the most part. And I got a real sense of satisfaction helping them find just the right dress or outfit for different special occasions. Since customers were always planning for a party or a wedding or another event, it always felt pretty festive in there. My favorite part was when someone would come in to buy a special occasion dress, and they'd be dreading the experience. But then I'd find something that made them look the best they could look, and they suddenly felt pretty and confident. That was the best."

Piper said, "Don't I remember that you went to school to get a job in fashion?"

Bibi made a face. "Yes. Good memory, Piper. It's too bad that nothing has gone right for me since I graduated with a degree in fashion merchandising. I've had a tough time finding work. I'm not sure I had a grasp on what I was going to do with my degree. I probably thought I'd go up to New York and try to get in with a designer." She snorted. "Good luck with that. There are way too many other people with fashion merchandising degrees for that to work. Then I ended up here, in Dappled Hills. Came to visit a friend and never left."

Beatrice asked, "Did Mona let you help with some of the buying? I'd think it would be great to get a younger person's perspective when purchasing clothing for the boutique."

Bibi shook her head sadly. "Nope. I'd have *loved* to help with the buying, too. But Mona only wanted that to be her department." She shrugged. "I guess she did have a good handle on what her customers wanted."

"Did you ever ask her to help with the buying?" asked Piper.

"I did once," said Bibi ruefully. "And I regretted it. Mona thought I was overstepping. Plus, she got super-defensive like she thought I might be trying to take over the shop or something. She was a bit of a control freak."

Beatrice asked, "What did you think about the clothes Mona selected for the shop?"

Bibi quirked a brow at her. "Let me ask you the same question, first, since you were in there shopping. Did you like the clothes?"

Beatrice considered this. "Well, I wasn't shopping for myself. It's a little different when you're shopping for a friend. My main impression was that everything was very expensive." She paused. "Did I understand correctly that Mona expected her staff to wear clothing from Mountain Chic?"

Bibi rolled her eyes. "You got that right. Isn't that unbelievable?"

Piper shook her head. "That's crazy. I know those clothes cost a ton of money. Did she give you a discount?"

"Not much of one. She took the cost of the outfits out of my paycheck." She looked at Beatrice. "To answer your question, I did like the boutique's selection—for an older woman. Mona didn't stock anything that was cutting edge, of course. Nothing that was currently hot in the fashion world. She mostly picked elegant, classic clothes. I thought she might be able to have more sales if she offered a wider range of styles, especially in different price ranges."

"I'm guessing Mona didn't like that idea," said Beatrice dryly.

Bibi grinned at her. "You guessed right. She thought she'd stick with specializing for a specific customer. I wanted to push her on it, but it wasn't my shop. And now, it doesn't matter at all. I don't work there anymore, and Mona is gone. It's still hard to wrap my head around that fact. Mona was always such a huge presence there."

Piper said, "Do you have any ideas about who might have murdered Mona? Did she have any issues with anybody? Maybe, if there's another suspect, you'll feel like the police aren't paying so much attention to you."

"Good point. And I know just the guy to be a perfect suspect. Dillon Peters."

Piper asked, "Is that Mona's husband?"

"Sure is. And I have overheard plenty of phone calls over the months where Mona snapped at Dillon. Or yelled at him. I mean, raising her voice to the point where I worried the customers were going to hear her. Or even the folks at the restaurant next door."

Beatrice asked, "Why was Mona so upset with her husband?"

"Well, lots of things. She thought he was lazy, bad with money, drank too much, and wasn't supportive enough. But the biggest thing is that Mona accused him of having an affair."

Piper raised her eyebrows. "And she'd yell all that stuff at him while people were around?"

"Yep. Oh, she'd try to be discreet at first. Mona would always close the door to her office. But then she'd get all wrapped up in their conversation and sort of lose her mind. She'd raise her voice. The customers would be so taken aback by it. It embarrassed me. I never knew whether to acknowledge it was going on, or whether to pretend I couldn't hear her. It was so unprofessional."

Piper asked, "Do you think her husband was actually having an affair?"

"Who knows? But Mona sure thought he was. She was upset about it, but it sounded like the main reason she was mad was because it would make her look bad. Like the spurned woman or something." Bibi shrugged. "Maybe Dillon didn't do it. It could have been the other woman. Maybe she came to the shop to have it out with Mona and things got out of control."

Beatrice asked, "Did Mona know who the woman was?"

Bibi nodded. "She said her name, often, in a sneering voice. Said that if he was going to have an affair, the least he could have done was to pick someone with a little class. Her name is Kendra Callan."

Piper said, "Hmm. I don't know that name at all."

"If she's as unclassy as Mona was saying, you probably wouldn't."

Beatrice said, "Piper, Kendra is actually in my Pilates class. The one you go to from time to time."

"Ohhh. Got it. I remember her now."

Bibi looked at her watch. She said to the little boy in the swing, "Tyler? We need to head back home. Your mama is going to be coming home in a few minutes."

Tyler, who'd been nodding off with the gentle swinging, woke up and raised his arms to be picked up. Bibi stopped the swing and lifted him, setting him carefully back down on the ground again. "It was good talking with y'all," she said. "Sorry that you had to hear me ranting over all this. I haven't had anything on my mind but Mona, and you can definitely tell. But I feel better, though, talking about it."

"Glad it helped to talk it out a little. Good luck with the job search," said Piper.

Bibi gave them a wave as she left the park, holding Tyler by the hand.

Chapter Six

"Wow," said Piper. "That was a lot."

Will wanted to get out of the swing too, now that Tyler was done. After Piper lifted him out, he trotted over to the sandbox. Piper pulled some toys out of a bag she'd brought with her. Will immediately started playing with the different trucks, making pretty accurate truck noises as he did.

Beatrice said, "It sounds like Bibi is really having a tough time finding another job right now."

"I know. And the last thing I need is a babysitter. Not with two eager grandmothers at the ready," said Piper with a laugh.

"Oh, Meadow would kill you if she had to share Will with yet another person," said Beatrice. "She thinks it's bad enough that she has to divide her time between me and Miss Sissy."

Piper nodded. "Maybe Bibi will find something soon. I feel bad for her." She paused. "I don't know Bibi well, but I got the feeling she wasn't telling the truth about why she was fired."

"I thought the same thing. Maybe the real reason she was let go is embarrassing or something. Josh at the restaurant seemed to think Bibi had done something wrong. But it could have simply been that Mona was very picky about how her staff per-

48

formed. Maybe Bibi didn't take direction well or something minor like that. Obviously, I didn't know Mona. That's not exactly the type of place where I shop." Beatrice looked ruefully down at her daily uniform of khaki pants and a button-down top.

"Exactly. And it's way too dressy for me to wear at the school or when I'm on the playground. Plus, Bibi's right—Mona specialized in clothing for older women. And women with plenty of extra money to spend."

Will said something to Piper that Beatrice couldn't completely understand. Piper, on the other hand, seemed to know exactly what he wanted. "Snacks? Sure. You're hungry?"

Piper reached into her bag and pulled out some sandwich bags with various crunchy snacks in them. She made a face. "I don't know, these seem really unappetizing to me right now. What do you think, Mama?"

Beatrice thought the snacks looked pretty crumbly and like they'd been in the bag for a while. "Maybe you need to refresh your snacks. In the meantime, how about if we eat out? My treat. I know we had those grilled cheese sandwiches, but apparently, I'm hungry again. At least, I'm hungry enough for an appetizer or a dessert or something."

Will was starting to fuss. Piper said, "That would be absolutely awesome. I need to head off the tantrum I see coming. But even if I head that off, I'm not sure he's going to be great inside a restaurant."

"There are outdoor tables at Josh Copeland's restaurant. Will can watch all the goings-on up and down the street. That could be distracting enough to keep him happy for a while."

Piper lifted an eyebrow. "Josh Copeland's, hmm? Right next to the boutique. Might you be thinking of doing some investigating?"

"Only in the most subtle way possible," said Beatrice with dignity.

They gathered the toys, shook the sand off them, brushed the sand off Will as much as possible, and then headed across the street to the restaurant. It was quiet there, and the few diners they had were eating inside.

"Perfect," said Piper with relief. "It's always less-stressful when a restaurant isn't packed, especially when I'm not sure about Will's mood."

"Sunday dinner at home is still a real thing in Dappled Hills," said Beatrice.

The hostess spotted them and seated them right away at a table right by the sidewalk. Sure enough, Will was watching a couple of people walking a large dog down the street.

"Excellent!" said Piper. "Maybe this will occupy him for a while."

A minute later, Josh Copeland came out with a laptop and set up in a shady spot under the awning. When he spotted Beatrice, he waved and came right over.

"How are things going?" he asked. "I'm guessing you're having a better day than you did yesterday, at any rate?"

"For sure," said Beatrice. "And I get to spend some of it with my grandson and my daughter, Piper."

Josh, in full outgoing, marketing mode, beamed at Piper and extended his hand for her to shake it. "Such a pleasure to meet you, Piper. What a beautiful boy you have."

Will gave him a solemn look. "Eat," he said.

Josh nodded at him. "You've come to the right place for that, young man." He looked at Piper. "Chicken fingers? A fruit cup?"

"Chicken fingers would be great," said Piper with a smile.

Josh motioned one of the servers over and gave him the order. He turned back to Beatrice and Piper. "That way Will can get served first while the two of you peruse the menu."

He glanced next door at the boutique and grew visibly tense. "I do wish they'd finish up next door. The police are taking up some of the parking spots. I need every spot I can get." He sighed. "The lack of parking and the police presence are definitely affecting business. I don't have nearly as many diners here as I usually have on a Sunday."

"Parking is key, isn't it?" asked Beatrice, leading Josh on.

He jumped on her statement with alacrity. "Isn't it? Nobody thinks about it, but it's vital. People want an easy spot where they can hop out of the car and find something to eat. They don't want to circle the block a million times or park a quarter of a mile away. That's very stressful." He huffed. "It's been tough to protect my spaces. Mona's customers had absolutely no courtesy whatsoever. They were all acting extremely entitled."

"I wonder what's going to happen to Mountain Chic now," said Piper.

Josh shrugged. "I can't see Mona's husband running it. If he closes the shop, I'd love to lease that spot. I could expand the restaurant then."

Beatrice wondered if he'd mentioned this salient point to the police. It definitely seemed like yet more motive. She made a mental note to contact Ramsay and let him know.

"What was Mona like?" asked Piper. "Her shop was out of my budget range and I don't think I ever met her."

Josh seemed to be trying to temper whatever it was he was about to blurt out. After careful consideration, he said, "Well, I think she ran her shop with excruciating care. Details were things that seriously mattered to Mona. She also wasn't great at delegating. I went over one day to talk to her about our parking problem, and she was completely distracted. Her employee was folding a stack of knit tops, and Mona swooped in, jerked the tops out of her hands, and folded them herself. I ended up leaving, I was so irritated. It was clear she wasn't going to listen to a word I said."

Will's chicken fingers arrived at that point, and Josh stopped talking, looking across at the shop next door with irritation. After the server left, he leaned forward, peering closer. "That's Dillon Peters over there. Mona's husband."

Beatrice glanced over. Piper was busily cutting up Will's meat into smaller pieces. Dillon was standing on the sidewalk outside Mona's shop, looking anxiously at the proceedings. He was a dark-haired, fairly nondescript man of average height and build.

"Wow, he looks terrible," said Josh. "Like a train wreck."

Dillon was pale and agitated, pacing on the sidewalk.

"You ladies mind if I invite him over?" asked Josh. "I can put him at another table, of course."

Beatrice quickly said, "Oh, he could sit with us. It looks like he could use a distraction. The baby can be the distraction."

Will gave his grandmother a solemn look at being called a baby. She leaned over, gave him a snuggle, and said, "I meant 'the big boy.'" Will smiled at her.

Josh stood up and walked over to Dillon. He pointed up at Beatrice and Piper's table, and they waved back. Dillon nodded slowly and joined them.

"We were so sorry to hear about Mona," said Piper immediately. "Won't you join us? I'm Piper and this is my mom, Beatrice. And my son, Will."

Dillon managed to give them all a rather sickly-looking smile. While he got settled at the table, the server came over and took Beatrice's and Piper's orders.

Josh pushed a menu at Dillon. "You have something to eat and drink . . . on the house."

Dillon looked absently at the menu as if not completely sure what it was.

Josh said. "How about meatloaf? You like meatloaf? Sure you do. Everybody does. We've got a great meatloaf."

Dillon nodded and Josh fired off an order to a somewhat jumpy-looking waiter who'd been hovering nearby.

Josh immediately launched in. "Dillon, I'm sorry about what happened to Mona. You know that, right? I mean, Mona and I had our differences. I'm not saying that we didn't. But I had a lot of respect for her and the way she ran her business. A *lot* of respect. How are you holding up?"

The answer was evident, though. Dillon wasn't holding up well at all. Will, carefully eating his chicken fingers, regarded him with concern.

Dillon shrugged, pushing a lock of dark hair out of his eyes. "I don't know, Josh. I guess I'm not doing so well."

"A shock, wasn't it? A terrible shock." Josh momentarily stopped speaking, looking impatiently around him. "Can we get this man something to drink? Where's drink service?"

The same jumpy server hurried over.

Josh asked Dillon, "Coke? Water? Gin and tonic?"

Dillon swallowed. "Gin and tonic might be good."

Josh had an expression on his face that stated he figured it might be. He waved his hand at the server, and the guy hurried off.

Will was still staring very seriously at Dillon as if not quite sure what to make of him. To keep him from staring, Piper pulled a coloring book and some crayons out of her bag. He started coloring in broad strokes over the entirety of a picture of Thomas the Tank Engine as he munched on his chicken. Beatrice particularly liked that he'd been creative enough to color Thomas in orange, instead of the traditional blue. It made it look very lively.

"So, how's it going, man?" demanded Josh to Dillon. "Are the cops giving you a hard time? The husbands are always blamed for this stuff, aren't they? Well, you'd know. You're a lawyer. I bet they've been giving you the third degree. Do you think they've pegged you as the main suspect?"

Beatrice couldn't decide whether Josh was trying to be supportive of Dillon or eager for any gossip he could hear. Josh's face was intent, his eyes unwavering on Dillon's.

Dillon put his face in his hands, maybe to avoid Josh's penetrating gaze. "I don't know," he said, his voice cracking. "I'm not sure if the police are giving me a hard time or if they're treating me like any other suspect."

"What kind of questions are they asking you?" pushed Josh.

Dillon shrugged, lifting his head out of his hands. "They've focused a lot on my actions yesterday morning. Plus my frame of mind. They particularly wanted to know where I was yesterday morning."

"Where were you? Do you ever go into the office on the weekend to catch up on work?"

Dillon sighed. "No. I was at home. Getting paperwork out of the way."

Beatrice thought this sounded very industrious for a Saturday morning. Particularly since Bibi had mentioned that Mona accused her husband of being lazy. Maybe Dillon had simply slept in, relieved to have some time apart from Mona while she was at the boutique. Although she didn't understand why he wouldn't tell the truth on such a small point. He didn't have an alibi, either way.

Josh snorted. "Well, an alibi of sitting at home and doing paperwork is not going to help you out at all. Anybody who can give you an alibi? Your lady friend, maybe."

Dillon turned even paler than he already was. Beatrice realized that perhaps that's why he'd lied about the paperwork. Maybe Kendra Callon had been at the house with him. Could he want to protect her instead of using her as an alibi? That seemed very gallant, under the circumstances. But then, Kendra might be married, too. Revealing his alibi, if she was one, would create all kinds of problems for her, if that was the case.

Josh made a shooing gesture at Dillon's horrified countenance. "Oh, don't worry about it, Dillon. Probably the only people who know about the affair are those of us at this table and whoever was close to the boutique when Mona was yelling at you on the phone. Mona was pretty loud when she talked on the phone, especially when she was talking to you, I guess. She forgot where she was, I think."

Dillon said slowly, "Okay. That's not good."

"Well, it's good if you get an alibi out of it."

Dillon shook his head. "She wasn't over then. I really was doing paperwork by myself. I'd gotten seriously behind on my billing and the office was giving me a hard time over it."

Josh sat back in his chair, giving him a look of pity.

The server hurried up to the table, carrying a tray with Dillon's gin and tonic and the food for Beatrice and Piper. Dillon eagerly grabbed the drink, taking several thirsty gulps. He gazed down into his drink for a few moments. "You know, I still cared for Mona. I wanted to make things right with her. That's what the police don't seem to understand. It's like they've created their own narrative of what's happened, and they're not considering other possibilities. The more they investigate me, the less time they're spending finding out who actually murdered Mona."

Josh said, "Absolutely. Of course, they've still got to focus on you as a suspect. Since you were the spouse and everything. And might not have had the most solid marriage."

Dillon acted as if he were arguing a case. "Mona was actually a wonderful person. She was always interesting to talk with. She had ideas about any subject. They weren't just ideas, either—she read a lot and knew stuff about all kinds of things. And Mona was so organized. Oh my gosh, that woman was so organized. Not only was she organized, she was *motivated*. She knew how to get stuff done in the quickest, best way possible." His voice trailed off as if he couldn't think of anything else nice about Mona.

"Being a lawyer and hanging out in the courthouse all the time, you probably know the cops in this town pretty well, don't you?"

Dillon nodded, but didn't look too hopeful.

Josh snapped his fingers. "Oh, wait. You're a defense attorney, aren't you? Yeah, I guess you and the cops look at things pretty differently. If you were a prosecutor, you'd at least be on the same side, right?"

Dillon took another large sip of his gin and tonic. Josh motioned to the nervous server for him to bring Dillon another.

Josh said, "Have you ever socialized with the cops, though? Christmas parties, things like that? Do they have things like that at law firms?"

Dillon's meat loaf arrived at the table then. He stared at it as if it had come from outer space. He finally said, "Uh, I was never that sociable with the police officers."

Josh nodded. "Got it. That's a pity." His eyes opened wide. "Hey, have they been through and searched your house and everything? I guess that would be one of their first steps, wouldn't it? I bet you made sure their warrant was in good shape!"

The server slid the other gin and tonic in front of Dillon. He picked it up and knocked back half of it in a practiced manner. "They've been by the house, of course."

A smile played on Josh's face as he watched Dillon. "I guess the best thing for you to do is find somebody else to blame. Right? If there's another suspect, that will help take the attention off of you."

This statement made Dillon rally a little. Or maybe the alcohol was speaking. "You and Mona weren't exactly friends."

Beatrice and Piper glanced at each other. Even Will stopped coloring Thomas the Tank Engine at the change of tone. But the way Dillon said it made it seem more like bravado and less like he actually believed Josh might have murdered his wife.

Josh blinked and then let out a belly laugh. "Okay, okay. You came out swinging with that one. But let's face the facts here, Dillon. You have a lot more motive than I do. You were in an unhappy marriage. You were having an affair! Or maybe Mona knew too much about you and whatever she knew was going to impact your legal business. Could something like that be it?"

Dillon drained the dregs of the gin and tonic and set it back on the table with a thump. "Whatever. You're simply deflecting." He paused. "Mona told me about a problem she had with her quilting club—guild, whatever it's called." He glanced at Beatrice and Piper as if they could help fill in the blanks.

"The Cut-Ups," the women chorused.

Dillon nodded. "Yeah, that's it. Mona wasn't the kind of person who went to all the meetings or events or anything, but she'd been going to more of them lately. At the club."

"The guild," said Beatrice.

"Right, yes. The guild meetings. Anyway, Mona told me that one of the quilters was stealing supplies from the storage closet."

Beatrice and Piper glanced again at each other. They hadn't heard anything about this.

Dillon continued. "The group meets at a church, I guess, and the church lets them have their own closet to put extra fabric, books, and other supplies in there. Which was pretty generous of the church, actually, to give the guild the meeting space and storage, too. When Mona found out that this woman was stealing in a *church*, though, it made her see red. She wasn't stealing *from* the church, just from the guild, but it was the setting that made her so mad."

Josh snorted. "That's the kind of thing that would drive Mona crazy, for sure. She was a stickler for everybody following the rules. Did Mona call the cops on the woman?"

"Mona was threatening to. The woman was apparently upset and was trying to persuade her to forget about it. I tried to calm Mona down, but she wasn't having it. She was very indignant about the stealing, but that's not a surprise. Mona always did have a well-developed sense of fairness and justice."

Beatrice cleared her throat, and Dillon looked at her in surprise, as if he'd nearly forgotten she was there. "How many people do you think Mona told about the supply closet theft?"

Dillon thought about this for a moment. "I'm not really sure. I would have paid a lot more attention if I'd realized it was going to be important. But at the time, it was Mona complaining about yet another thing. Mona often complained about stuff." He frowned, still thinking. "I remember she mentioned that she told the president of the club. But she wanted to let the police and other people know. Maybe whoever this woman is decided to kill her before she could say anything and ruin her reputation."

It certainly sounded like a plausible motive.

Josh waved his finger at Dillon. "I know another suspect, too. That woman that Mona fired. The girl who worked at the boutique."

Dillon frowned again as if trying to dredge the name up from his memory. "Glenda?"

"No. Not that one. She was a couple of employees ago," said Josh.

Dillon shrugged. "Marsha?"

"I think she was last year."

Dillon sighed. "I had a hard time keeping up with Mona's employees. She went through them like Kleenex. But like I said, Mona was totally organized and knew what she wanted. If the employee wasn't delivering, she was out of there."

"The girl was Bibi," said Josh with a smile. "She's the one Mona fired just recently."

"Mona might have mentioned her, but I don't remember anything specific. I'd have paid a lot more attention if I'd known how significant this stuff was going to be. Wish I could help you out, but I can't."

Apparently feeling better after finding at least one suitable alternate suspect, Dillon finally dove into the meatloaf.

Will had finished with his chicken fingers and with the coloring, too. The street scene was also starting to get a bit old. He wriggled in his seat and said, "Home."

"Want to go home, little guy?" asked Piper. She glanced at her mother. "Are you ready?"

Beatrice nodded, reviewing the bill and putting the amount and a tip on the table. She said to the two men, "It was good sitting with you. We're very sorry about your wife, Dillon."

Dillon gave her a weak smile back. Still, he looked better than he had when he'd sat down with them. The alcohol had provided two streaks of vibrant red on his cheeks.

Josh said, "Thanks for coming by. Come back anytime."

Chapter Seven

A few minutes later, they were walking back home. Piper said, "Well, that was a lot more of an interesting meal than I thought it would be."

"For sure," said Beatrice. "Dillon seems to be an anxious mess right now, but who can blame him?"

"I got the feeling he might have something of an alcohol problem," said Piper. "Did you?"

Beatrice nodded. "I did. He had a very practiced manner of tossing the drinks back. And he was a little too eager to get them in the first place. I realize he's going through a terrible time right now, but it seemed he might be doing a lot of drinking, regardless."

"That's what I thought, too."

Beatrice got a text message. "It's Meadow. She's come up with some snacks as options for Tiggy's and Dan's reception, and she wants me to taste test them." Beatrice rubbed one of her temples. "I'm not sure if I have the appetite or the patience for that right now."

"Not feeling much in a Meadow mood?" asked Piper with a smile.

"Not so much. But I should probably do it. Otherwise, she'll keep haranguing me about it. You know how she doesn't give up when she's got a project."

Piper said, "I surely do. How about if I drop you by there, instead?"

So Piper drove the short distance from Beatrice's to Meadow's house.

Beatrice said with a teasing grin, "Want to come in and say hi to her? I know she'd love to see Will."

Will had been in danger of falling asleep in the car on the way back. Any catnap would mess up the main event nap, though, and Piper had kept him awake by having the windows down in the backseat.

"Nope! No way, ha. Tell her I said hi and that I'm taking Will home for a well-deserved nap. I might even have one myself."

Beatrice gave her a hug and hopped out of the minivan. When she tapped on the door, Meadow sang out, "Come in!"

It all looked rather chaotic inside. Boris leaped around happily, giving her doggy grins, and clearly delighted to see her. Meadow was wearing a "kiss the cook" apron that was covered with flour. It looked as if Meadow had taken out every pot and pan she owned and placed them in various locations on the counters and tabletops. The little dog, Cammie, was looking around her with a rather disgusted expression on her tiny face.

"Welcome to the circus," said Ramsay dryly. Beatrice hadn't even noticed him at first, with all the chaos everywhere else. He was wearing his police uniform and a wry expression.

"Came home for a bite of something to eat and was presented with a tasting menu," he said with a sigh. "I don't think I gave Meadow the feedback she was looking for."

"You certainly did *not*," said Meadow sternly. "I needed the food rated by taste, portability, and wedding appropriateness."

Ramsay nodded. "Good luck," he said to Beatrice. "You're going to need it."

Ramsay quickly left as Meadow said, "That Ramsay! He's always so dramatic."

Beatrice thought Ramsay was probably the least dramatic person she'd ever met, but smiled at Meadow. "Okay, so what have we got? And just a heads-up: I've eaten two lunches today already."

"Excellent! So you're actually on a roll then, food-wise."

"Well, I guess you could put it that way," said Beatrice. "Although it's more apt to say that I have a full stomach."

"These are just tiny, delectable morsels," said Meadow. "They definitely won't fill your stomach up any more than it already is."

Beatrice wasn't sure that was technically possible, but nodded her head in acquiescence.

"And while you're here," continued Meadow sweetly, "you can tell me all about what happened at the boutique."

Beatrice gave her a knowing look. "I see. This isn't about trying your tasting menu at all, is it?"

"It most certainly is. You know I value your advice."

Beatrice said wryly, "I know that *you* know that every morsel you bake or cook is delicious. I believe you've gotten me here under false pretenses."

Meadow snorted. "You've clearly been spending too much time with Ramsay. You're even starting to sound like him. Okay, I admit it. I somehow didn't hear about poor Mona until last night."

Beatrice stared at her. "How is that even possible? Did you drive out of town directly after Posy's program?"

"I was listening to music here at the house and trying out a bunch of different ideas for the reception food. Then I was talking on the phone to Tiggy and Dan about what kind of food they might want to have."

Beatrice was relieved to hear that Meadow had actually thought to consult the bride and groom over the matter. She'd seemed determined earlier to forge her own way when it came to the wedding reception. But Beatrice was still confused how Meadow hadn't heard about Mona. "Tiggy is Georgia's aunt."

"Right as always, Beatrice!"

"Georgia was with me when we discovered Mona. How did Tiggy not tell you on the phone?" asked Beatrice.

Meadow flushed a little. "Oh. Well, I might have been driving that conversation just a smidge. I jumped right into the subject of food. There was lots and lots to talk about. I sort of launched right in."

Beatrice suspected that Meadow had actually completely hijacked the conversation with Tiggy and Dan. If Tiggy had even tried to broach anything about a murder at the boutique, Meadow would have likely started vaguely musing on the possibility of crepes at the reception.

"Before I tell you what happened yesterday, why don't you end my suspense and tell me what the bride and groom decided in terms of food," said Beatrice.

"A pasta buffet." Meadow's face was pleased. "Inexpensive, easy to prepare, and tasty. I think it sounds like a winner."

"And I know you're excellent at preparing Italian food. So the tasting menu today is . . . what?"

"Oh, little nibbles for the dessert portion."

Beatrice said, "But I know we'll have wedding cake for dessert. June Bug is coming up with some magnificent creation. And her wedding cakes taste *wonderful*, not like cardboard like so many others do."

"And she's going to do an absolutely amazing job! But there's always room for more sweets, don't you think?" She shoved a plate at Beatrice, filled with tiny portions of brownies with Oreo frosting, miniature lemon meringue pies, and white chocolate tartlets, among other diminutive treats.

"I'm going to explode," said Beatrice, staring at the food in front of her. "But at least I'll die happy."

Meadow beamed at her. "Take a bite of one, tell me *briefly* what you think, then tell me all about yesterday."

Beatrice reported on the tiny lemon meringue, which naturally, was delicious. "Well, right after the program was over, Georgia and I went over to the shop next door so Georgia could see if there might be anything there for Tiggy for the wedding."

"Gracious! She still hasn't settled on a dress, then?"

"I think it took a while to dissuade Tiggy from making the dress, herself. Now she's at the stage where she needs something immediately. Preferably something that doesn't need altering.

Anyway, we went inside and weren't having much luck finding a suitable dress for Tiggy," said Beatrice.

"I could have told you that. The clothes in there are outrageously expensive. Plus, I know it's terrible to speak ill of the dead, but Mona was a very condescending saleswoman. I stuck my head in one time, just to tell her about an upcoming quilting event, and she quickly told me she didn't have anything in the store to fit me." Meadow huffed. "I wasn't even asking her!" Meadow, who was big-boned and well-proportioned, but always looked great, still seemed irritated.

Beatrice shook her head, feeling steamed on Meadow's behalf. "I'm sorry she was so ugly to you. You're the perfect size. She had no right to speak to you that way."

"Thank you, Beatrice. As you know, I've never put a lot of time or effort into what I wear or how I do my hair. I like clothes that make me feel happy." She gestured down to her wildly colorful, if mismatched, clothing. Meadow always loved "flowy" clothing, as she called it. Today, she had on a billowing tie-dye tunic in riotous, swirling colors. Below the tunic, she wore a pair of wide-legged patchwork pants. To complete the look, she wore a pair of well-loved sandals sporting colorful beads that made soft jingles when she walked. "The stuff in Mona's shop wouldn't have made me feel happy, comfortable, or confident."

"I know what you mean. You'd have been stultified in those clothes. Many of them were pretty corporate-looking. Needless to say, we weren't having any luck. We walked to the back to check out the sale section, but there wasn't anything there that would work as Tiggy's wedding dress. I spotted Mona on the floor, right as we were turning to leave."

"What a terrible thing," said Meadow. "I may not have been Mona's biggest fan, but she was one of our own!"

"In what way?" frowned Beatrice. She was quite sure Mona wasn't one of *her* own, at any rate.

"A quilter, silly. Although she didn't participate as much as she could have. That's why I was always trying to encourage her to go to various programs and shows. Although, I stopped doing that after she was so snippy when I went to her shop."

"Understandably. Anyway, we called Ramsay, and he came right over. Josh, the restaurant owner from next door, came straight over, too," said Beatrice.

"I do like that restaurant," mused Meadow. "The Sunflower Grille, with an 'e' at the end, just to make it fancy. His Italian dishes are excellent. He has a vegetarian lasagna that's to die for. I wonder if I should visit to get some ideas on my pasta buffet."

"I doubt you need any ideas. You'll be fine. I think you could create an amazing pasta buffet in your sleep."

Meadow said, "We'll see. Okay, sorry for interrupting. What did you hear from Josh?"

"Well, Ramsay knew that Josh and Mona had been on the outs a lot. They squabbled over parking places and the music Josh's restaurant played on his patio. It sounded like one or both of them had called the cops on the other a few times."

Meadow sighed. "That's not very neighborly, is it? You'd think that all the downtown businesses would be trying to support each other, wouldn't you? Help each other out. So Josh and Mona had issues with each other. Do we think Josh had something to do with Mona's death?"

"Who knows? He definitely had a motive over the parking issues. I'm guessing the altercations were escalating, since the police were getting involved. It would also have been very easy for him to slip away, murder Mona next door, and go right back to the restaurant with no one the wiser."

Meadow said, "A terrible thing for him to do. Imagine getting that upset over parking places!"

"I'm not saying he did it, but I'm sure Ramsay is considering him as a suspect. Speaking of Ramsay, he didn't fill you in on all this?"

Meadow snorted. "As if! He'd called me, saying he had a new case, and he'd be missing supper. He ended up coming in after I fell asleep and left this morning before I even woke up. He finally mentioned Mona, and the fact you and Georgia had found her, when he came home for lunch a bit ago. He didn't offer any additional information, except that you might know more details. He's been most annoying."

"Well, the police have really been camped out at the Mountain Chic boutique. Piper and I ate at Josh's restaurant after going to the playground this afternoon." Beatrice stopped short, mentally kicking herself. She hadn't meant to tell Meadow that.

Meadow put her hands on her hips. "What? You, Will, and Piper went to the playground after church today? And didn't invite me?"

"It was a very spur-of-the-moment thing. Plus, you've been so busy with your wedding planning." Beatrice gave a shrug that she hoped said it all.

Meadow grunted. "I suppose that's true. Okay. Well, next time, make sure I'm there. So, the restaurant? You were talking with Josh again."

"We were. But more interestingly, Mona's husband, Dillon, came over."

Meadow's eyes grew wide. "Did he? He's got to be a major suspect, being the husband and all. How did he look? What did he say?"

"Dillon looked absolutely awful. I don't think he'd gotten a bit of sleep last night. Apparently, he's a lawyer, so I guess he knows he might be in some trouble."

"I'll say." Meadow shook her head.

"Dillon was also having an affair, according to Bibi and Josh. They both heard Mona yelling at Dillon on the phone about it."

Meadow gave a humph. "Well, that's certainly even more motive. He wanted to get rid of Mona so he could start a new life with the woman he's having the affair with."

"But why kill Mona? Why not divorce her? If he's an attorney, money shouldn't be an issue."

Meadow said, "Dillon could have lost control in the moment and lashed out. Who knows? Anyway, I'm sure Ramsay is looking pretty hard at him. He's always said it's the people we know best who are the most dangerous."

"Josh was pushing Dillon, trying to make him think of someone else who could have murdered Mona. He was thinking that would be a good way for Dillon to get himself off the hook."

Meadow snorted. "And Dillon probably said Josh had plenty of motive."

"That's exactly what he said at first. But then Dillon started talking about a quilter."

Meadow's eyes narrowed. "A quilter? That sounds extremely unlikely. Who?"

"I don't think Dillon knew her name. All he knew was Mona had accused a member of the Cut-Ups of stealing from the guild's supply cabinet."

Meadow put her hands over her mouth, her eyes wide behind her red framed glasses. "Thea."

"You know about this?" Beatrice wasn't sure why she was surprised. Meadow did usually know all the gossip around Dappled Hills. That's because she'd lived in the area her whole life and knew just about everybody and just about every*thing* about everybody. Which is why it had been so surprising that she hadn't heard about Mona's murder.

"Unfortunately. I have to say that Mona was being ugly, from all accounts. She was threatening to call the police on poor Thea. I heard Betty Cantrell tell me all about it. Mona was also saying she was going to tell everyone in the guild about it. That word would spread that Thea was a thief and couldn't be trusted." Meadow's eyes glinted with anger.

"I don't understand. So the Cut-Ups meet in a church and the church has given them use of a supply closet. They're keeping their extra fabric and sewing machines and whatnot in there?"

Meadow said, "Exactly. Just to keep things convenient for the group. I have the feeling that, if Thea had *asked* for some fabric, no one would have had a problem in the world giving her some. From what I understand, Thea absolutely adores quilting. It's the one thing that keeps her going and happy during dark days. But she doesn't have any money. What money she saved up was drunk by her no-good husband. Fortunately, she was able to divorce him, but the divorce took money, too. So here she is, practically destitute, with no money for the very quilting that gives her joy and purpose."

Meadow, as expected, was getting pretty fired up. Beatrice had the feeling that one of Meadow's "projects" was about to be birthed. Thea was sure to be taken under Meadow's wing, despite Meadow's involvement in lots of other projects, including an upcoming wedding.

Meadow continued, "This is how I see it. Thea, in her need for quiet quilting, took a bit of fabric from the closet. Maybe some notions. Maybe she was planning on replacing the supplies later on. But Mona either caught her red-handed, or saw her acting suspiciously and figured it out."

Beatrice asked, "Did Mona *see* Thea take the supplies?"

Meadow threw her hands up in the air. "Who knows? Mona was the kind of woman who had eyes in the back of her head. Mean eyes."

Beatrice shook her head. "Unfortunately, this doesn't look good for Thea. Mona originally had just told Betty Cantrell about the theft, right? She hadn't told anyone else?"

Meadow nodded her head. "That's right. Betty is the president of the Cut-Ups right now. She started her term a month or so ago. That's why Betty called me up to feel the whole thing out. She wasn't sure how to handle it."

Beatrice continued. "But Mona also threatened to let the rest of the guild know. And the police. That's not good, Meadow. It means that Thea had plenty of motive to kill Mona. Thea isn't in the position to spring back from those kinds of accusations. If word gets out that she might be a thief, it could even jeopardize her employment."

Meadow knit her eyebrows. "That Ramsay won't pick on Thea. Not if he knows what's good for him."

"It's his job, Meadow. And I'm sure it's going to come out. It doesn't mean that Thea did it, but she'll have to be cleared. Maybe she even has an alibi."

Meadow looked a bit more cheered at this. "That's true. Maybe she'll immediately be eliminated from his inquiries. It's the *last* thing that Thea needs right now. She works at Bub's Grocery. You know how the management is over there. It's just like you said—it could jeopardize her employment. If they get even a whiff that Thea might be involved in any impropriety, she'll be out the door."

Meadow snapped her fingers. "I know what to do." She picked up her phone and dialed a number, then waited impatiently for someone to pick up. "Hello? Is this customer service at Bub's? Good. I'd like to speak with a manager, please."

Meadow was abruptly put on hold. Beatrice could hear the jazzy hold music from where she was sitting. Beatrice took a bite of one of the desserts and closed her eyes. Sweet perfection, for sure.

A manager apparently answered because Meadow said, "Yes, I wanted to tell you something about one of your cashiers. Thea Owen."

The manager said something that made Meadow scowl.

"What?" she asked. "No. I'm not complaining about a thing, for heaven's sake. I'm calling to say that Thea does such a *marvelous* job. She always has a sweet smile on her face and asks how I'm doing. It genuinely brightens my day to shop in Bub's. That's right. I simply wouldn't know what to do if she weren't working there."

"Oh, she'll be working tomorrow morning? Wonderful. I'll look forward to doing some shopping then. You have a nice day, too." Meadow hung up, looking pleased. "Thea works tomorrow morning. You and I have a mission."

"Don't you already have a plethora of missions?"

Meadow said, "Not so many that I can't help a quilter in distress." She paused, frowning in thought. "You know what else we should do? As a guild, I mean? We should raise a little money or contribute some from our general funds to have supplies for women who can't afford them. And not just for our area—maybe we can spread the word and other guilds can build up their supply closets."

Beatrice nodded. "That's not a bad idea. Of course, you'll need to publicize it a bit. I would think there might be plenty of crafters in the mountains who might be able to use a little help with fabric."

Then Meadow was off and running with the topic. She dialed Posy to tell her about the idea. Beatrice finished her taste testing, jotting down notes on the back of one of Meadow's grocery lists.

Meadow hung up, looking pleased. "We're going to do it. It's officially going to be a Village Quilters project."

"That's wonderful," said Beatrice. She patted her stomach. "I'd better head home while I can still walk. I'm completely overloaded with food now."

"Did you finish your tasting menu?"

Beatrice nodded, pointing to the scrap of paper. "They were all delicious, Meadow, as you knew they would be. I made a few notes there."

"Got it. Well, thanks for coming by. And tell Wyatt I said hi."

"Will do," said Beatrice.

"And I'll pick you up at nine tomorrow morning."

"Nine?" asked Beatrice, confused. "For what?"

"To speak with Thea, silly! We were just talking about it. She works at Bub's tomorrow morning. We're going to go over there on the pretext of shopping and then ask her some questions. Maybe we can even catch her during her break. That would be especially nice."

Beatrice wasn't at all sure that *Thea* would think it especially nice. Not when she was trying to eat, hydrate, and possibly visit a restroom during a short break. But she nodded and waved goodbye as Meadow's phone rang again.

Chapter Eight

The next morning, Beatrice rose early. If Meadow was going to hijack her morning in any way, it meant that she'd better get everything done she needed to get done beforehand. This meant finishing a load of laundry, dead-heading her knockout roses outside, and putting together the all-important grocery list which was their excuse for being at Bub's to begin with.

"Do you need anything from the store?" Beatrice asked Wyatt.

"Hmm? Oh, I thought that was a ruse to speak with Thea."

"It is, and it isn't. I believe Meadow thinks it will give us more legitimacy. That we won't be skulking around the grocery store, tying up cashiers with conversation," said Beatrice.

Wyatt nodded. "I see. In that case, I'd love it if you could pick up one of those trail mixes."

Beatrice's eyes twinkled. "Now I get it! You're the one who's responsible for the strange disappearance of the trail mix I picked up last time."

Wyatt gave her a remorseful look, and she reached out to hold his hand. "No need to look so penitent. I'm glad you liked it."

"Maybe you should pick up *two* containers this time. I started eating them and decided they would be perfect to take to work. That way I could have something healthy to eat in the office when I got hungry. I meant to tell you that I took them, but I totally forgot."

Beatrice chuckled. "That's totally fine. I figured it was either you or Noo-noo, and I'm glad it was you."

Wyatt left for work a few minutes later, and Meadow showed up moments after he left.

"Ready?" she beamed at Beatrice. "Have your shopping list?"

Beatrice waved it in front of her.

"Then we're off!"

Beatrice got into Meadow's car and they set off for the grocery store. Bub's had been around for what looked like a couple of hundred years. It was the only place in Dappled Hills to shop, and they knew they had a corner on the market. The prices were probably a bit higher than they should be and the selection was limited, but everything a shopper got there was good quality. Rocking chairs sat in front of the wooden building and a collection of elderly men hung out there as regulars: chatting, telling stories, and watching the world go by.

Meadow said, "Now, I know I'm horning in on your sleuthing. But if I didn't go, you wouldn't even know which cashier Thea was."

Beatrice lifted an eyebrow. "It's not as if Bub's employs a slew of cashiers. She might be the only one there at nine in the morning."

Meadow seemed blithely unconcerned about this fact. "Anyway, I'll be your helpful sidekick. I'm sure there might be various angles we'll want to question Thea on. The more we know, the more we can help! And Thea desperately needs our help. Clearly."

They walked through the creaky doors into the timeworn shop. Meadow darted around the grocery store on the warped wooden floors, obviously a lot more familiar with its contents than Beatrice was. Beatrice had gotten hung up at the trail mix section on the snack aisle. There were more varieties and brands than she'd remembered. Usually, Bub's just had one or two options for each category of food. But there must have been ten different trail mixes. That must have something to do with the fact that there were often hikers in the store.

Meadow caught up with her. She stared at Beatrice's empty cart in disbelief. Meadow's own cart had about twenty items in there, and she'd even carefully checked off each one on her grocery list. "What happened?" she asked incredulously.

Beatrice sighed, gesturing at the shelf. "Trail mix happened. Wyatt liked what I'd bought him last time and asked for more. I didn't remember there were this many choices, especially at Bub's. Omega-3 trail mix, protein-packed trail mix, raspberry, and chocolate . . ."

Meadow reached out and plucked down a sweet and salty mix, barely glancing at the container. "This is the one you should get."

Beatrice looked doubtful. "I'm not sure that's the one Wyatt liked so much."

"Trust me. Ramsay is a trail mix aficionado, and this is his favorite mix. If Wyatt doesn't like it, you can drop it by our house. But I know he will. Ramsay eats a couple of these a week. I buy them up and store them in our pantry when they go on sale."

Beatrice took the trail mix and put it in her cart. It looked tiny in the huge cart.

"Might better get two," said Meadow, putting another one in the cart. "Now, what else is on that list of yours?"

Beatrice stared at it. "Well, I need to go to the cereal aisle."

"Let's divide and conquer," said Meadow. She reached out, plucked the list from Beatrice's hand, tore it in half, and hurried away with the other half.

"It's not like we're in any rush," said Beatrice to Meadow's retreating back.

"Break time is in five minutes," she called back. "I asked."

Meadow was finished with her half of the list far before Beatrice was. And when she caught up with her, she'd actually found all the correct items. Beatrice had figured that Meadow wouldn't know exactly what she wanted, but she seemed to have an unerring instinct for grocery shopping. Beatrice quickly finished by grabbing the final two things on her list. Meadow and Beatrice checked out at the front. Thea was nowhere to be seen.

"Where do you think she took her break?" asked Beatrice.

"They told me there was a little eating area out in the shade at the side of Bub's," said Meadow. "They thought Thea might be out there."

And sure enough, a few moments later they found Thea there. She was a small woman with mousy brown hair falling gently around her face and a skittish look about her, as if she might flee from any given situation at a moment's notice. She wore a white Bub's tee-shirt, khaki pants, and a nametag. Beatrice realized she seemed to be crying.

Meadow swooped right in like a mother bear. "What's happened, Thea? Has the grocery store been ugly to you?" Her eyes narrowed, a look which boded ill for Bub's Grocery.

Thea shook her head and sniffed. Beatrice took a packet of tissues from her purse and handed them to Thea, who took them gratefully. After gently blowing her nose a couple of times, Thea took a deep breath. "I feel so awful about Mona." Her thin shoulders were slumped as if she were carrying a heavy, unseen weight.

Beatrice and Meadow exchanged a look. There were many ways to feel awful about Mona. Was Thea feeling awful she'd murdered her? Or awful that Mona died?

After a moment, Meadow said, "Of course you do! Mona was in the Cut-Ups with you. Our quilt guilds are like sororities, but better. We support and love each other."

Thea looked miserably at Meadow. "I *wish* I'd loved Mona. Instead, I've been so relieved she's gone. I feel so wicked thinking like that. The guilt is eating me up."

Meadow patted Thea on the back in a flurry of pats, almost as if she were a baby that needed to spit up the guilt she felt inside.

Beatrice cleared her throat. "That's completely understandable, Thea. From everything that I've heard, Mona could be a very difficult person to get along with. No wonder you feel that way."

Thea gave her a grateful look. "Thank you. I just don't want anyone to think badly of me. Something happened between Mona and me . . . something bad. When she died, the only thing I could think of was that her death solved a problem for me." She shook her head. "I can't seem to shake that feeling."

"Do you want to talk about what happened between you and Mona?" asked Beatrice in a quiet voice.

Thea hesitated. "Part of me really does. If I could get it off my chest, I would. I haven't slept the last two nights since Mona died. But if people heard about this stuff, they'll never look at me the same way again."

Meadow said briskly, "I'm sorry to tell you this, Thea, but word is already out. I hate to alarm you, but there it is."

Thea's eyes grew big. "Oh no. Someone talked."

"Well, it might even have been Mona. She doesn't seem to have been the type of person who kept things under her hat very well," said Meadow. "What might work better now is if you tell us about everything. Put your own spin on the story. People need to hear your side of what happened and not make judgments."

Thea considered this for a moment before slowly nodding. "Okay. And believe me—I was just trying to stay out of Mona's way. I hoped she'd let it go and forget about it if she didn't see me around. I'd never have done anything to hurt her . . . to hurt *anybody*."

"Of *course* you wouldn't," said Meadow.

Beatrice wasn't so sure. It was definitely hard to picture Thea taking on a woman as tough as Mona was. But when someone was cornered and desperate, there was no telling what they might do.

Thea took a deep, shaky breath. "Okay. Well, I know I don't have a lot of money, but you have to understand I would never steal from the guild."

Meadow nodded. "I'm sure you wouldn't. By the way, I was wondering if the Village Quilters might create a supply closet like the Cut-Ups have. Posy might have a little space for us in her back room at the Patchwork Cottage. What sorts of things do the Cut-Ups have in theirs?"

Thea grew more comfortable answering this soft ball of a question. "It's stuff we might need for quilt shows or guild meetings. There are banners with our guild name on them, extra fabric, books on quilting and stuff like that." She paused, looking down at her scuffed-up tennis shoe. "Mona acted like everything was so organized in the closet that she could tell when something was missing. But it wasn't like we had any sort of inventory sheet or anything in there."

Beatrice said, "So Mona *guessed* you had stolen something from the closet."

Thea flushed. "She saw me in there and misunderstood what she saw. I was seeing what kind of fabric was in there. Then I'd have asked the president if I could buy it at a discount. But Mona accused me of sneaking in there and stealing it. She said she'd noticed earlier that there was fabric missing and figured I was there to steal from the closet a second time. She was going to announce it at the beginning of the next guild meeting." Thea trembled at the thought.

"Not a very charitable thing for her to do," said Beatrice.

Thea nodded. "She terrified me. If people think I steal things, I could lose my job here at the store. It's not a great job or anything, but it's the only way I can put food on the table right now. I went through a divorce and a bunch of other stuff and *need* this job." She sighed. "And part of me kept thinking that Mona always acted like she was absolutely perfect." She hung her head. "It's so bad to talk about the dead."

Beatrice and Meadow shook their heads, wanting to hear what Thea had to say.

"Okay. Well, I'm usually quiet. I spend a lot of time listening to other people and folks' kind of forget that I'm around. Anyway, that's how I overhear things. I was here at Bub's, restocking shelves a week ago. Sometimes they have me restock when things are quiet at the store. I heard Mona's husband, Dillon, and Kendra Callan talking in the snack aisle."

Meadow leaned in a little, nodding.

Thea slowly continued. "Dillon wanted to leave Mona. He was telling Kendra that."

Meadow's eyes opened wide. "I can't believe they'd talk about that kind of stuff in public."

Thea said, "Oh, you know. They were being pretty discreet. They weren't holding hands or kissing or anything. And people who work at the store are practically invisible to most people."

"What else did they say?" asked Beatrice.

Thea considered this. "Well, I could tell they worked together. I guess Mona's husband is a lawyer? And Kendra is too. At least, that's what it sounded like." She looked anxiously over at us to see what we thought.

Meadow said, "She's absolutely a lawyer. Wills and estates, I think."

Thea said, "Got it. They said anybody who saw them together in public would think they were out shopping for a working lunch. The store wasn't busy. Nobody would have overheard them if it hadn't been for me."

"What did Kendra say when Dillon mentioned leaving Mona?" asked Beatrice.

"Her voice is softer, so I couldn't really hear what she said. I'm sure she was so happy, though," said Thea in a wistful voice. "And Dillon sounded so in love—like all his dreams were coming true." She looked down at her scuffed shoes again. "Anyway, so Mona wasn't as perfect as she always seemed. I figured if her husband was so relieved to leave her, they couldn't have the best marriage. I know all about that from experience." She frowned and checked her watch. "Break's over. I've got to go."

"See you later, Thea," said Meadow. "Hang in there."

Chapter Nine

Beatrice and Meadow got back into Meadow's car after they loaded their groceries in the back. "Gracious," said Meadow. "It does seem as if there's lots of drama going on in Dappled Hills."

"As usual," said Beatrice dryly.

"I'm trying to think what I know about this Kendra. I was able to pull the fact that she was a lawyer out of my head, but that's about it."

Beatrice said, "As a matter of fact, I might know more about her than you do this time, which is very unusual. Kendra happens to be in my Pilates class."

"Really? I didn't realize you were taking a Pilates class." Meadow didn't seem outraged this time over not being included in the activity. That's because exercise, unless it was gardening, housework, or walking Boris and Cammie, was anathema to her.

"It's over at the church. Ginger decided to start up the class. I started going just to support her, because seven p.m. on a Monday seemed like a horrible time to have an exercise class. But I've ended up getting a lot out of it. Piper comes sometimes too when Ash is home from work."

Meadow quickly said, "I'll call Piper and assure her I'd love to watch Will for her on Monday nights so she can go." She paused. "Maybe starting after the wedding."

Beatrice wasn't surprised in the slightest to hear this. "I'm sure she'll appreciate it."

"Are there many people who come?" asked Meadow idly.

"There are usually about ten of us. I think that's pretty popular for a small town and that time of day. I'll be sure to make it tonight."

"I still think it was brazen for Kendra and Dillon to be discussing their personal affairs in the grocery store," said Meadow. "Imagine."

Beatrice shrugged. "I guess it didn't matter if someone overheard them if Dillon was on the verge of divorcing Mona, anyway."

Meadow pulled into Beatrice's driveway and put her car into park. "Do you think Kendra might have approached Mona for some reason and killed her?"

"Well, Bibi said Mona stated that Kendra wasn't classy, but I can't imagine that extends to murder."

Meadow frowned. "If she's a lawyer and does Pilates at church, she sounds plenty classy to me. Maybe that was just Mona's idea of a put-down that would irritate Kendra if it got to her ears."

"Maybe Kendra really *did* get irritated and went over to Mona's shop to have it out with her. Things could have gotten out of hand." Beatrice paused before mentioning that Mona had been strangled with a scarf. She had the feeling Ramsay hadn't mentioned the cause of death to Meadow, since Meadow was fond of gossiping. But strangling someone seemed very much like an impulsive, angry action to Beatrice.

Meadow nodded. "Same with Dillon." She looked as if she had more to say, but Beatrice was ready to get inside the house. Plus, Noo-noo was looking out the front window at her, grinning a fetching doggy grin.

"I better put away this ice cream," said Beatrice quickly. "Otherwise, it's going to end up as a puddle in your car."

Meadow apparently didn't fancy that. "Okay. See you later. If you find out anything, let me know."

The only problem with letting Meadow know anything was that she had a terrible time keeping things quiet. Beatrice decided that it would be a much better idea to let *Ramsay* know. In fact, there were already a few things she felt she might need to clue him in on. She made a mental note to do that later. After getting back from the grocery store expedition, the rest of the day passed fairly quietly. Beatrice put away her groceries, then drove Noo-noo to the park to set out on the trails that connected with it. They took a long walk so the little corgi could stretch her legs and Beatrice could think things through.

When they got back home, Beatrice sat down to do some work on her mixed media quilt. Handling her mother's things was a relaxing activity in itself, and working on a craft made it even more so. She had a beautiful, intricate lace handkerchief that her mother had made for the center of the quilt, a bit of tulle from her mother's wedding dress, and some of her vintage button collection. The mixed media teacher had encouraged them to make pockets to hold paper items, and Beatrice was planning on putting her mother's recipe cards in one or two of them.

She settled down to read her book in the hammock in the backyard. Noo-noo, still a bit tired from their long walk on the trails, settled down next to her. She'd filled the bird feeders a couple of days ago and the sound of birdsong was also relaxing. Beatrice and Noo-noo quietly watched chickadees, nuthatches, cardinals, and little hummingbirds zipping back and forth to the feeders.

Beatrice shouldn't have been surprised, after the walk, the quilting, and the reading in the hammock, that she fell asleep, but she was. When Wyatt came back from the church and found her and Noo-noo snoozing, she was startled to find that she'd slept for over an hour.

"Mercy!" said Beatrice, struggling to sit up. "I didn't mean to nod off."

"You must have needed the sleep," said Wyatt sympathetically. "Considering everything that happened on Saturday, it makes sense."

"What time is it?" asked Beatrice, trying to peer at her watch, which had slid around her wrist.

"Six o'clock." Wyatt's voice was apologetic, as if he knew this news was not what she wanted to hear.

"Mercy on us!" said Beatrice again. "I need to get us something to eat. And my Pilates class is coming up in an hour."

"I'll put together some food. And you don't *have* to go to Pilates. You could skip it this time."

Beatrice said, "I'll take you up on the cooking. But I did want to make that class."

Beatrice got into her exercise clothes while Wyatt made a quick inventory of the contents of the kitchen. When she joined him in the kitchen, he'd made them both omelets.

"I hope breakfast for supper is all right," he said with a smile. "I didn't think I had enough time to cook the baked potatoes, which was the other option."

"This is perfect." Beatrice gave him a kiss. "Thanks. I'll cook next time. You shouldn't have had to come back from work and fix something."

"You know I don't mind doing it. I was sitting at my desk and in meetings a lot today and it was good to be on my feet and doing other things."

They ate together, talking about their days. Beatrice looked at the clock. "I'd better head over."

"Want me to drive you there and back? It'll be dark when you get out."

Beatrice said, "No, I'll be fine. It's such a short walk. Besides, it serves as a little warm-up for my class."

A few minutes later, she was on the church grounds and heading to the room where the Pilates group was held. Inside, there were nearly a dozen women, and the mats were set up and ready to go. The instructor spoke with Beatrice before the class started.

Beatrice was glad to see that Kendra was one of the women in attendance. She was an attractive woman in her late thirties who had one of those engaging laughs. But Beatrice noticed she seemed quiet and appeared to be keeping to herself. When the class started, Beatrice noticed Kendra was looking her way.

Once the class was over, Beatrice saw Kendra didn't linger to speak with anyone, but hurried out the door. Beatrice put her mat away, thanked the instructor, and left to walk back to the house. She cut through the church parking lot to get to the road.

Kendra, seeing her, motioned her to a quiet spot away from the other cars. "Hey there," she said in a tight voice. "I was hoping to get a chance to speak with you."

"Is something wrong?" Although Beatrice knew there was.

Kendra gave a short laugh. "Right now, it seems like everything is wrong." She paused. "I heard you were the one who found Mona."

"Well, I was one of the ones, yes. A terrible thing. Did you know Mona well?'

Kendra sighed. "Beatrice, I've done something I shouldn't have done."

Chapter Ten

Beatrice froze, thinking for a second that she might be about to hear a murder confession.

Kendra continued. "I was having an affair with Mona's husband, Dillon. I feel terrible talking about what I did, especially here on church grounds, of all places."

Beatrice smiled at her. "Well, confessing at churches is sort of a given, isn't it?"

At this, and the note of kindness in Beatrice's voice, Kendra broke down. "Sorry," she sobbed.

Beatrice said, "And I'm sorry I don't have any tissues with me."

Kendra gave her a shaky smile. "I came prepared." She pulled a tissue out from the pocket of her exercise pants. She shook her head. "I feel horrible about everything. I'm married, Dillon was married. I don't know what we were thinking."

"You want to stay with your husband?" asked Beatrice quietly. The other women from the class were walking to their cars and looking at them curiously.

"I do. I just got sort of swept up in this affair. I was flattered, I'm sure. And it was a break from the humdrum reality of life. Dillon started talking about leaving Mona and marrying me."

Beatrice asked, "And that's not what you wanted to happen?"

"Actually, it *is* what I wanted to happen. At the time, that sounded completely perfect. Like that was going to be the rest of my life." Kendra gave another short laugh. "I must have been dreaming. And now I'm in a nightmare. Mona is dead, I'm a suspect, and I'm having an affair with a coworker that has to stop."

Beatrice asked, "Have you tried ending things with Dillon?"

"I *want* to end things. I feel even worse about our relationship now that Mona has been murdered. Plus, I remember the reasons I married my husband . . . reasons I conveniently forgot when Dillon and I started seeing each other."

Beatrice said slowly, "Dillon didn't seem very well the last time I saw him. He was very shaken up. Have you seen him?"

"I haven't seen him since the day before Mona died. Since Friday." Kendra paused. "Beatrice, did you get the impression when you saw him that he might have something to do with Mona's death?"

Beatrice quickly said, "I don't know Dillon well enough to be able to read his emotions. All I know is that he seemed exhausted and very stressed. That could be from any number of reasons."

"Like being a suspect in a murder inquiry," said Kendra wryly. "Can you tell me more about what happened with Mona? The police didn't give me much information."

Beatrice didn't want to divulge anything sensitive, so she covered what she thought most people probably knew already. "Well, we found Mona in the late morning. We didn't see anyone leaving the shop or hanging around there."

"Were you able to tell how she died?"

Beatrice thought about the cheery scarf that had been used to murder Mona. "No," she lied. "But the police immediately considered her death suspicious."

Kendra looked at Beatrice as if she wasn't entirely sure she believed that Beatrice didn't know the cause of death.

Beatrice asked, "Do the police know about your connection with Mona?"

"Oh yes." Kendra made a scoffing sound. "I guess there really aren't any secrets in Dappled Hills. They knew about it right away. That's the whole reason I'm a suspect. I'm sure somebody saw or heard something and immediately rang up the police."

"That must have taken you by surprise."

Kendra shook her head. "Not really. Any bit of surprise I felt was immediately overcome with the realization that I needed to be as upfront as possible with the cops. They would have found out about the affair for certain at some point, and it was better for me to control the narrative."

"You probably know the police, I'm imagining."

Kendra said, "Ramsay? For sure. I see him pretty frequently. And I am even familiar with some of the state police. Ramsay has always seemed smart and fair. Sadly, I don't have any sort of alibi, so I couldn't help myself along too much. I'd taken the morning off from the office for a hair appointment."

"That sounds like an alibi to me. The salon could verify to the police that you were there."

Kendra sighed. "Yes, but then my beautician called Saturday morning to cancel because she'd woken up sick. So instead of just going into the office, I decided to sleep in and then hang around the house."

Beatrice said, "You asked earlier if Dillon might be upset because he had something to do with Mona's death."

Kendra looked down. "I didn't mean that. I can't imagine Dillon would do anything to hurt Mona. Or *anybody*. He's always been sort of strait-laced. Having an affair seemed totally out of character for him."

"Do you know what kind of relationship the two of them had?"

Kendra said, "Well, it wasn't a good one. I'm honestly not sure why Dillon would have wanted to marry Mona to begin with. Or vice versa. I guess Mona might have been attracted to the fact that Dillon was an attorney."

"Was money important to her?"

Kendra shrugged. "The same as it is to anybody, I suppose. Appearances were more important to her, from what I could tell. I think she might have liked her status in town. She wouldn't have liked Dillon trying to divorce her, that's for sure." She paused. "Statistically, husbands are usually responsible in a situation like this. Clearly, Dillon's marriage wasn't a very happy one or he wouldn't have had an affair to begin with. He would talk about how abrasive Mona was—that she couldn't let things go. She'd yell at him when he didn't do things exactly the precise way she wanted things done."

"But that's not a real motive for killing someone," said Beatrice.

Kendra gave her a wry look. "Isn't it? From my years studying law, I've read about people getting murdered for far pettier reasons. It sure doesn't take a lot for some people to fly off the handle and kill someone close to them. You'd think it wouldn't be that way—that most murders would be committed by strangers. But that simply isn't the case. Statistically, we're much more likely to be murdered by someone we know."

"Did Dillon ever talk about other people who might have been upset with Mona? Anybody else who could have had a motive? Family? People she knew from the boutique? Friends?"

Kendra nodded. "Definitely. As I mentioned, Mona had that abrasive personality. I told the police they should take a closer look at Josh, the restaurant owner next door to the boutique. I believe they were already speaking with him. Everybody knew the trouble those two caused for each other. Again, it was all petty stuff, but they got very angry over it."

"And they were having public arguments about it. At least, that's what someone mentioned to me."

Kendra quirked an eyebrow. "It had escalated beyond mere public arguments. Josh let the air out of Mona's tires on one occasion. Mona retaliated by keying Josh's car. Mona had been considering filing charges against Josh after the tire incident. But Dillon realized Mona was just as much at fault as Josh had been. Dillon told her if she called the police (which she'd done on other occasions), Josh could file a charge against her, too. That made Mona back off, at least for a while."

Mona sounded like someone who was fond of threatening to call the cops. She'd apparently done the same thing when she accused Thea of stealing supplies from the guild's closet. Beatrice wondered if it were because Mona liked the feeling of putting someone in a scary situation. Maybe she was the kind of person who liked power trips.

Kendra continued. "It's a mess, isn't it? The more I've thought about it, the more I've felt tainted by association." She glanced behind her at the church. "I've noticed when I come here, even to exercise, it's like a sanctuary." She smiled at Beatrice. "No pun intended."

"I feel the same way," said Beatrice. "You should come over more often. We have a lot more to offer than just Pilates."

Kendra nodded. "I've been thinking about doing some volunteering here. I haven't been feeling too good about myself lately and volunteering might be a way to feel better. And give back at the same time, of course. Do you know of any opportunities that might be coming up in the evenings? Or even any nighttime church activities, period?"

"There are Bible studies in the evenings, several nights."

Kendra didn't seem all that interested in Bible studies. "I was thinking about something more hands-on."

"Wednesday night is a busy time here. We can always use extra hands for food set-up, clean up, and things like that."

Kendra was apparently something of a picky volunteer because she didn't seem very interested in that, either.

Beatrice pulled up the church calendar on her phone. "It looks like the clothes closet needs help sorting clothes next Tuesday. It's the kind of activity that shouldn't be too taxing, even after a full day at the office. It's in the late afternoon, around 5:30."

Finally, she'd hit on something that seemed appealing to Kendra. "I'll check that out, thanks. And thanks for listening to me, Beatrice." She paused. "Are you walking home? I could give you a lift."

"Oh, I'm right next door. It's good to stretch my legs."

Kendra quirked her brow again. "I thought we'd just done that in class."

So Beatrice ended up accepting a very speedy ride home with Kendra. She thanked her, and Kendra waved and kept on her way.

Wyatt had the front light on and was at the door before she could get her key out to unlock it. He looked relieved to see her. "I was starting to worry about you."

She gave him a hug and a light kiss. "I should have texted you to let you know I was held up at the church."

"Was there a problem there?" asked Wyatt with a frown.

She shook her head. "Kendra Callan wanted to speak with me after class. She was giving me some insight into her thoughts on Mona and Dillon and Mona's relationship. Which reminds me that I need to call Ramsay and fill him in on a few different things." Beatrice glanced across the room at the clock and grimaced. "It's later than I thought it was. Maybe I should wait until morning."

"Isn't Meadow a night owl? You could text her to see if Ramsay is available."

Beatrice nodded. "Good idea." She took out her phone and texted Meadow. Meadow immediately answered her. "She says

Ramsay just got back home for some food and can talk to me."
She dialed Ramsay's number, and he quickly picked up.

"Hey there, Beatrice," he said, sounding like he was swallowing down a meal. "What have you got for me?"

"Sorry to bother you while you're trying to eat. I can talk to you tomorrow, if that's better."

Ramsay said, "No, this is fine. I'm eating some of the little bites of Meadow's tasting menu, so they go down pretty easily. Tell me what's on your mind."

"Well, basically I wanted to do a brain dump with you. I feel like I've been talking with a lot of people, and I don't want to know something and not realize I know it."

Ramsay said, "Good idea to call me. You definitely shouldn't put yourself in any sort of danger."

"Right. I understand you know about Kendra Callan's relationship with Dillon Peters?"

"Their affair?" asked Ramsay. "Yes."

"It's hard to really get a read on how serious it was, but one of the cashiers at Bub's Grocery said she overheard Dillon saying he was going to leave Mona to marry Kendra."

Ramsay was quiet on the other end of the line for a few moments. "That's very interesting. I was under the impression from Dillon that he had no interest in continuing that relationship with Kendra. That he'd thought the affair had run its course."

"Maybe he's trying to minimize his motive for killing his wife. Kendra is married, of course. It didn't sound like she was planning on leaving her husband. Plus, she was asking questions that indicated she might be suspicious of Dillon." Beatrice paused. "Is Meadow around?"

"She's stepped outside to let Boris out."

"Okay," said Beatrice. "Then it's a good time to tell you that one of the quilters in the Cut-Ups might have had a good reason to murder Mona."

Ramsay groaned. "Oh, no. It's never good when a quilter is a suspect. Meadow will go after me if she thinks I'm giving the woman a hard time. Who is it?"

"Do you know Thea Owen?"

"Thea Owen, Thea Owen. Doesn't she work at Bub's? Is she the one you said overheard Dillon saying he was going to divorce Mona?"

Beatrice said, "She's the very one. But she had her own problems with Mona. Mona accused Thea of stealing quilting supplies out of the Cut-Ups' storage closet in the church. She'd told the guild president about it already."

Ramsay gave a low whistle. "Seriously?"

"Yes. Thea denied it. But apparently, Mona was threatening to go to the police. Thea was worried about losing her job at the grocery store. Apparently, she's in dire financial straits after her divorce. Plus, she wouldn't have wanted that kind of information to get out around town. When I spoke with Thea, she said she was planning on asking the guild if she could buy the fabric from the Cut-Ups at a reduced rate . . . that she hadn't been stealing or planning to steal anything. In her view, Mona had completely misconstrued what she'd seen."

"Got it." Ramsay's voice was grim. "Okay, thanks. We'll be checking into that."

"There was also some other stuff I heard about Josh and Mona's battles. But I understand you already knew about it."

Ramsay asked, "Oh, you mean the car wars? Letting air out of tires and keying cars? Yes, I'm aware of all that, even though no one called the police. There were witnesses in the parking lot who called it in. Mona and Josh didn't even look around to make sure no one was watching when they vandalized the other's car. Neither one of them was a master criminal. Those two definitely hadn't been acting like adults. Honestly, I wouldn't have been shocked if *Josh* ended up as the victim and *Mona* as the main suspect. She wasn't exactly crazy about that guy." He paused. "Anything else?"

"Josh told me that he was hoping Dillon closed Mona's boutique so that he could lease the space and expand his restaurant."

Ramsay said, "Is that so? Well, that certainly sounds like another motive to me. And Josh has quite a few of them already. Anybody else you talked to?"

Beatrice ran through all the different people she'd spoken with. Josh and Dillon, Kendra and Thea. She'd forgotten about Bibi.

"I did talk with Bibi Norton when Piper and I were at the playground with Will," said Beatrice.

"Did you? The playground seems like an odd place for Bibi to be hanging out. From what I heard, she's single and doesn't have children."

Beatrice said, "She's babysitting right now, so she had one of her young charges with her. Since Mona fired her, she's had a tough time finding work. She offered to babysit for Piper, as a matter of fact."

"No thanks. I'm not saying Bibi had anything to do with Mona's death, but I don't fancy my grandson being babysat by a murder suspect," said Ramsay flatly.

"There is that. Piper also mentioned she had a few too many local grandparents to need any outside help with babysitting."

"That's the truth," said Ramsay. "Meadow would foam at the mouth if she lost any chances to spend time with Will. What else did Miss Bibi have to say?"

Beatrice hesitated. "Well, she said that Mona fired her because Bibi was asking for too much time off from work."

"But your tone says you didn't completely believe her."

Beatrice said, "I didn't. There was something about her manner. I wondered if Mona had fired Bibi for something significantly more serious. Something that, if it was known, would impact her job prospects."

"Something like theft?" asked Ramsay. "Maybe Mona thought Bibi was stealing merchandise?"

"Maybe. Although that would be quite a coincidence, since Mona had already accused poor Thea of theft."

Ramsay said, "It sounds like Mona's general modus operandi. She might just have been paranoid about people stealing from her. Probably comes with the territory when you own a high-end shop."

"Maybe. Bibi is having a tough enough time finding work as it is. It would be even harder if Mona had spread word around that she'd done something underhanded."

Ramsay asked, "Did Bibi say anything about who she thought might have been responsible for Mona's death? I know who she told *me* who she thought would be a suspect, but I'm curious if she named anybody else to you." He proceeded munching again on Meadow's tasting menu items.

"She mentioned Dillon. Bibi overheard a lot of one-sided arguments between the two of them. Mona was apparently particularly upset about the affair between Dillon and Kendra Callan. Bibi said Mona was calling Kendra low class."

Ramsay snorted. "That's rich, coming from Mona. Being classy does not entail keying someone's car or yelling at your husband over the phone where customers and employees can overhear you. Anything else? You've got some good stuff here."

Beatrice thought for a few moments. "No, I think that's probably about it. Just a lot of people with very negative encounters with Mona."

"Sounds about right. Now for something completely off-topic before I run back to the station. What are you reading? I've got a great book for you."

Ramsay and Beatrice had established a reading buddy relationship. Ramsay was something of a more adventurous reader than Beatrice was, but he'd also encouraged her to read some great books that she wouldn't have picked up otherwise. She liked to think that she'd done the same for him. Beatrice knew that Ramsay was longing for the day when he could stop policing and start reading and writing full time.

"I've got to find something new to read, actually. I'm thinking about heading to the library tomorrow and re-reading a Rosamunde Pilcher book. I'm in the mood for a comfort read, and she's one of the best at those," said Beatrice.

"I've got one for you, if you're up for it."

Beatrice asked, "A comfort read?"

"Well, not so much a comfort read. Just a *good* read. Although I do like Rosamunde Pilcher, too. I'm reading something by Cormac McCarthy right now."

Beatrice said, "No way. I'm in no frame of mind to be reading *The Road* or some other brutal book."

"It's not *The Road*. It's *The Crossing*, and it's magnificent," said Ramsay.

Beatrice was somewhat doubtful. "I'm sure it is. But having discovered a body on Saturday, I'm needing a novel that wraps me up in cotton wool and keeps me floating on a cozy cloud. Maybe I'll be ready for something different in a couple of weeks."

"I'll remind you again about it then," said Ramsay cheerfully. "In the meantime, though, I have an idea. You were telling me last week that you haven't read much modern poetry."

"Apart from yours, no. But I found yours very enjoyable. I like the way you can evoke images with a few, precise words."

Ramsay asked, "So what poets have you read in the past?"

"Well, there was Wordsworth, of course. He was practically a requirement when I was going through school."

Ramsay snorted in derision. "I can see why you didn't stick with reading poetry, if that's what you were reading."

"Oh, I don't know. 'Daffodils' was pretty. I memorized that in fourth grade. I can't remember what I did yesterday, but I bet I can recite that poem still."

"No, thank you," said Ramsay quickly.

Beatrice said, "Besides, that's not the only poet I read. Yeats was much better. 'The Second Coming' was powerful. And actually, I was very fond of Longfellow's poems, especially those for children."

"And Robert Frost?" asked Ramsay.

"Sure. In high school. I liked 'Death of a Hired Man.' And some Langston Hughes in college. Good stuff. But aside from that, I haven't spent much time reading poetry."

Ramsay said, "I have a poet for you. Billy Collins. Modern—still living, as a matter of fact. He writes amazing poetry about everyday things that make you look at life differently. To me, that's what poetry is all about. You could read one of his collections while reading your Pilcher novel."

"Have you got a book I can borrow?"

"I sure do. The only problem is that I wrote in it. A lot. There are tons of marginalia in that book. It might be a little distracting."

"Your copy of *Heart of Darkness* was like that, and I made it through all right."

Ramsay said, "As long as it doesn't bother you too much. I'll ask Meadow to drop it by the next time she's out. Okay, I'd better head back out. Thanks for the info, Beatrice. You take care out there."

Chapter Eleven

Beatrice was amazed to find that she was able to drift to sleep that night. Although she'd had Mona's murder on her brain, perhaps the nighttime Pilates had relaxed her enough that she was able to fall right into a restorative sleep.

She woke to find that Wyatt had apparently gotten up quite a bit earlier. He'd walked Noo-noo and made a big breakfast of eggs and waffles.

"Gracious," she said, rubbing her eyes and pulling her robe on as she joined Wyatt and a grinning Noo-noo in the kitchen. "I feel like Rip van Winkle, waking up from a long sleep. How long have you been up?"

"About an hour and a half. I knew you needed the rest. And Noo-noo and I had some together time."

The little corgi's grin grew wider. Beatrice suspected that Wyatt might also have slipped her a couple of dog treats. He knew she loved them.

"Have a seat, and I'll bring you a plate."

Soon Beatrice was at the table with a plate of steaming cheesy eggs and waffles in front of her. Wyatt gave her a big mug of coffee and a bottle of warmed syrup.

"I feel like it's my birthday," said Beatrice with a smile.

Wyatt sat down with her moments later, and they chatted about any number of things, none of them to do with murder, suspects, or dreadful discoveries in boutiques.

"Would you like to meet up with me for lunch today?" asked Wyatt. "I'm in meetings this morning and most of the afternoon, and a break in the middle of them would be great."

"That sounds perfect."

Wyatt asked, "Do we want to walk there? Or should I pick you up and drive?"

"Let's walk. Sometimes it's tricky to find parking at lunchtime. And, from what I've heard recently about squabbles over parking spots, it's just as well if we walk it. The weather should be beautiful, so that won't be a problem."

Wyatt said, "Sounds good. If it looks like the weather is changing, we'll drive for Plan B."

After Wyatt left, Beatrice did some housework and paid a few bills. She'd gotten into something of a rhythm with tidying the cottage. Tuesdays were her day to vacuum. Noo-noo gave her a wary look as if she was well aware it was Tuesday and the implications of that day. She wasn't at all fond of the vacuum and vacillated between chasing it unrepentantly to running away from it, room to room. Beatrice decided to give the little dog a break and put her out in the backyard. With the corgi's big ears, she could definitely still *hear* the vacuum, but at least the monstrous thing would be out of sight.

After the housework was over, she decided to run downtown to get the Rosamunde Pilcher book from the library. She knew she was going to be in the area of the library with Wyatt at lunch, but wanted to get started reading before then. She thought that might be a nice way to finish out her morning—in the backyard with Noo-noo and a book. Then she could read the book of poetry that Ramsay was lending her on the side whenever she ended up with it. That was the nice thing about poetry, she supposed. You could pick it up, put it down, and not even read the poems in order.

She drove to the library, checked out the book, and was soon back home reading in the hammock, a sleepy corgi with her.

After a bit, Wyatt came home, and they set off on foot to get lunch. Beatrice had been thinking they might go to the deli downtown and have a simple lunch of sandwiches. But Wyatt said, "All the talk about Josh's restaurant made me want to go there. Do you mind? I know you were just there."

Naturally, Beatrice didn't mind at all. The food was excellent, and she might even be able to find out more information from Josh. "No, that sounds perfect. A lot more relaxing than the deli. How has your morning gone so far?"

Wyatt made a face. "Well, it's not been as great as I would have liked. Remember how we polled the congregation to find out if they wanted the service times adjusted?"

Beatrice nodded. "To have the services earlier, later, or a combination of both."

"Right. Well, people apparently had lots of opinions about that," Wyatt chuckled. "Some folks didn't want anything at all to change and were pretty appalled that we'd even suggested it. Families with young children or teenagers were all pulling for later times."

Beatrice said, "Tricky. Did you and the church elders decide how to handle it?"

"We're going to put the matter up for a vote. The polling was to gauge interest."

Beatrice said, "Good idea. That way, the pressure is off the church leadership on the issue."

They reached the restaurant and decided to sit outside, since it was such a nice day. There was a cool breeze blowing, and the sun was in and out of puffy, white clouds. Beatrice decided then and there that she wasn't going to overstuff herself with lunch. It was the kind of day where, if she *did* overeat, she'd end up in the hammock, dozing, for the rest of the afternoon. While that didn't sound like a terrible fate, she did have some things she wanted to take care of at the house that afternoon.

A server quickly joined them, and they placed their orders early. Wyatt had already been thinking about the cheeseburger with hickory smoked bacon and pimento cheese. Beatrice, still mindful about the dangers of napping away her afternoon, chose the whole wheat veggie wrap with fruit on the side.

They chatted for a while, drinking fresh-squeezed lemonade and watching shoppers walking down the street in front of them. Their food came promptly, and they dug in just as quickly.

Wyatt closed his eyes happily as he took a bite of his cheeseburger. Beatrice grinned at him. "Is that what you've been waiting for?"

"Exactly what I needed. I haven't fired up our grill for a long time. I should do that soon. Maybe some shrimp and veggies or burgers. Maybe even steak."

"Let's not get too wild," said Beatrice wryly at the mention of steak.

They were finishing up when there was a shriek from inside the restaurant. Wyatt and Beatrice shared a concerned glance.

"I hope everyone's all right," said Wyatt slowly. "I wonder if someone had a medical emergency."

A moment later, they could hear sirens approaching the restaurant. "Uh-oh," said Beatrice.

Before the ambulance arrived, they saw Ramsay and some officers from the state police rushing into the restaurant from the station a few doors down. A few minutes later, Ramsay came out from the back of the restaurant, somewhat slower than he'd come in. He spotted Beatrice and Wyatt and walked over to their table. "Hey there. We're going to have to ask for everyone to leave the premises, but stay close. We'll need to speak with the diners later."

Beatrice frowned. This didn't sound like the medical emergency she and Wyatt thought it might be. "What happened, Ramsay?"

He lowered his voice. "Josh Copeland is dead."

Chapter Twelve

Soon, it was fairly chaotic outside the restaurant. Everyone had done as Ramsay had said and moved outside to the sidewalk, some diners still clutching their plates and eating lunch. The sidewalk wasn't very wide, so they were all leaning against the brick wall of the restaurant.

When Ramsay joined the group outside, his expression was a mix of weariness and concern. The diners all looked to him, and he said, "Unfortunately, there's been a suspicious death at the restaurant. I'm going to collect your contact information and let you go on your way. We'll be conducting a thorough investigation, of course, but initially, it appears the incident may have preceded any diners being here."

Ramsay's eyes scanned the group of diners. Most looked shocked. There was an older woman with tears in her eyes. He said gently, "If any of you do remember anything you think might be relevant to the investigation, don't hesitate to reach out."

Ramsay and his deputy moved through the group, collecting their information and giving tired reassurances to those who needed it.

When he reached Beatrice and Wyatt, he said with a sigh, "I'm afraid Josh had been deceased in his office for a little while. The door was closed, and the staff knew if Josh were working on the restaurant's books, it meant he didn't want to be disturbed unless it was a real emergency. Speaking with the diners wouldn't have been helpful under those circumstances."

Wyatt shook his head. "I'm so sorry."

Beatrice asked, "Do there seem to be any helpful leads?"

Ramsay said, "Not many. A knife was used this time, and of course this is a location with plenty of knives at a murderer's disposal. Either the killer wore gloves, or else they wiped down the knife afterward. No prints."

Beatrice said, "I wonder if Josh knew more than he was letting on. The restaurant is right next door to the boutique, after all. He was primed to be able to see something. And if he was in the habit of guarding the restaurant's parking spaces, he might have spotted Mona's killer."

"And not mentioned it?" asked Wyatt.

"Not if he were entertaining the idea of doing some blackmailing," said Ramsay. "I'm not saying that's what happened, but it's a possibility."

Ramsay's attention was suddenly diverted by a call from one of the state police officers. He quickly excused himself and headed off. Beatrice and Wyatt walked slowly away. The familiar charm of downtown Dappled Hills offered a bit of normality as they left the area, which was quickly becoming consumed by emergency vehicles. Wyatt reached out to hold Beatrice's hand, and she slipped it in his, feeling comfort in his presence.

Wyatt said, "I didn't know Josh well, but he always seemed so full of life and energy. It's hard to imagine that he's gone."

"It's hard for me to believe, too. Right in the middle of downtown Dappled Hills again, too. I wonder if Josh died because he stumbled across something he shouldn't have. Or maybe he heard something that led to this. It's all just such a waste." Beatrice shook her head. She thought of Mona, who had been a complex, difficult person, but loved her shop passionately. And Josh, who had been so lively, friendly, and interested in everything going on around him. Both of them should still be alive, still squabbling over parking spaces and enjoying the success of their downtown businesses. She sighed.

Wyatt cast a concerned look at his wife. "This week has been a tough one for you," he observed quietly, his voice laced with worry. "We didn't have the relaxing lunch that I was hoping we were going to have. Are you okay?"

"I'm going to be fine," said Beatrice with a wry smile. "I'm in a lot better shape than poor Josh is in."

"What are you going to do this afternoon?" He gave her hand a gentle squeeze.

Beatrice said, "I don't have any plans."

"You could go over and hang out with Meadow for a while."

Beatrice made a face. "No thanks. I believe I may have reached my Meadow quota for a while. She's been on a real mission with the wedding planning. You know how she gets."

"You could borrow Will from Piper." Wyatt was clearly trying very hard to come up with appropriate distractions from their disastrous lunch.

"It's Tuesday, so Will is about to leave preschool and have a nap." Beatrice smiled at her husband. "I'm going to be okay, really."

Wyatt was apparently ready to throw a hail Mary. "Do you have any interest at all in helping with the clothes closet at the church? Edgenora was telling me this morning that they needed a couple of extra people to sort clothes."

Edgenora was the stalwart presence at the church . . . the secretary who kept everything running smoothly. She was also the kind of secretary who would jump in to help out if there was a shortage of people for an activity, or to help set out folding chairs. She was definitely the glue who held it all together. Also calm and measured, she seemed to have boundless energy. The only problem with Edgenora hopping in to help with the clothes closet was that it took her away from the millions of other things she needed to be sorting out.

Beatrice said, "Actually, helping out sounds like the perfect idea. It's the kind of mindless activity that might be nice right now."

Wyatt looked relieved that he wouldn't be sending Beatrice back to a quiet house. "Good. Do you want me to drop you by the house, first? The clothes sorting is at two o'clock today. I know it's usually in the evenings, but the church had a huge influx of donations lately and they've piled up to the point that we need an extra sorting session."

"Sure. Drop me by the house for a second to let Noo-noo out, then we'll head over to the church."

Minutes later, Wyatt and Beatrice left their cottage and were pulling into the church parking lot.

"Let me know if you need me to give you a hand with anything," said Wyatt, still looking somewhat concerned about his wife. "There should be at least one other person helping in the clothes closet."

Beatrice smiled at him. "Thanks. I'm all good, though. I know you have an afternoon of meetings."

His eyes twinkled. "Trust me, I'd be delighted to be pulled away from one or more of them."

They headed for the church office. Wyatt's own office was located in the back. Edgenora sat at a large, organized desk and bobbed her head at them. She was on the phone, as she often was, fielding calls from members of the congregation.

Beatrice headed for a back room where a variety of different tasks were completed. Today it was the clothes closet, but the multipurpose room was also an impromptu meeting room, storage space, and place to organize Vacation Bible School in the summers. She was surprised to see Kendra Callan in the room.

"Hi there," said Beatrice with a smile. "What a nice surprise. I thought you would be at work."

It was just the two of them in the room, so Wyatt had been correct that the church needed help. There were overflowing boxes of clothes and no place to put them. The church served as a donation point before they shuttled the clothing to an agency that helped connect the clothes with people who needed them. The agency had itself been swamped lately and had asked them if they could sort the clothes by size and type before sending them along.

Kendra gave her a warm smile in return. "Hi to you, too. Yes, I'd ordinarily be at the office, but I decided to take the rest of the week off. I never take personal days, and I have tons of them saved up. I knew I wasn't going to be able to focus on work this week, not with everything going on. It would be better for me to go back when I can actually be effective. You'd mentioned the clothes closet sorting being in the evenings, but when I called the church office today to get more information, the lady said it was being done earlier today."

"That's what Wyatt was telling me. I'm glad you can take some personal days this week," said Beatrice. "I was telling Wyatt that this was a great mindless activity to keep your hands busy."

The door opened with a forceful creak and a gruff, no-nonsense older woman stomped in, glaring at them. "Need help?" she barked.

Beatrice remembered the woman as someone who put in a lot of volunteer hours at the church. She also remembered her as someone who was extremely deaf. She looked over at Kendra. "Do you think we need help?"

Kendra looked quite sure they didn't. Perhaps she wanted to speak with Beatrice in private. She wouldn't know that the old woman was so hard of hearing that anything they said would be private. "We're probably okay, don't you think?"

Beatrice said loudly, "We're okay. Thank you!"

The woman glared at her in response and stomped away.

Kendra made a face. "I hope we didn't hurt her feelings."

"She'll be fine. She prefers hanging out with Edgenora in the office, anyway. And Edgenora will have her making copies, doing filing, or doing any number of things."

Kendra said, "Good. Selfishly, I wanted to be able to talk with you alone, anyway. I've been thinking more and more about Mona's death. I've been trying to piece things together."

Chapter Thirteen

"Just make sure to tell Ramsay anything you think might be pertinent to the case. It's dangerous to keep things to yourself."

Kendra quickly said, "Oh, I will. Absolutely."

Something in her expression, however, made Beatrice wonder if that were true. She was about to tell her about Josh's death and warn her again when Kendra continued, this time on a different subject.

"On a completely different topic, I was wondering if you could tell me more about how leadership at the church is set up. I was thinking I might be interested in becoming more involved in church management."

Beatrice took a large pile of blue jeans and started sorting through them. "That would be great, actually. Wyatt is always saying we need more women in leadership positions here." She gave an overview of the Presbyterian church and how it was set up as a democracy, with deacons serving the role of representatives and elders serving as senators. In a matter of speaking, anyway. They were all elected by the congregation. Kendra became quite animated as they sorted, asking lots of questions. It was obvious that the set-up appealed to her.

Beatrice hesitated. "You're a church member, right?" She felt as if it was something she should know, but she had a hard time keeping track. Often, regular attendees hadn't gone through the membership process, but were just as involved as members were.

Kendra gave her a rueful look. "Not yet. And here I am, putting the cart before the horse, as usual."

"You should attend our new member class. It's a great way to meet other people, find out more about the church history, and learn about the different activities and groups we have. Plus, we have a new member class starting a couple of weeks from now. After that, if you like, you can join the church."

"That new member class sounds like it's starting at just the right time," said Kendra, folding a stack of white tee-shirts that she'd sorted by size. "Thanks for all the info. I'll get signed up. I've realized that the more time I spend here at the church, especially doing volunteer activities, the more I think about how I'm not getting a lot of fulfillment from my job as an attorney."

"I'm sure the people you're helping appreciate it."

"Oh, I'm sure they do," said Kendra. "But it's not meaningful work. I'm not saying it's not important to have a will or to think ahead on making decisions about your estate. But it's not like doing *this*." She motioned to the large pile of children's clothes, soon on their way to go to some kids who really needed them.

They worked quietly for a few minutes, getting the clothing into general piles divided by type of clothing before sorting them into sizes.

Beatrice said quietly, "Did you hear about Josh Copeland?"

Kendra frowned, knitting her brows. "Josh Copeland? You mean the guy who owns the restaurant downtown? What about him?"

"He was murdered sometime this morning," said Beatrice in a grim tone.

Kendra stopped short, staring at her. "You're kidding."

Beatrice shook her head. "I'm afraid not. Wyatt and I were at the restaurant when the staff realized what had happened and called the police."

Kendra sat down in one of the chairs. "I can't believe it. What on earth is going on? I'm sure the police think these crimes are connected, right?"

"I'm not sure exactly what they're thinking of course, but I'd imagine they are investigating the murders as linked."

Kendra was quiet for a few moments, thinking. She gave a short laugh. "And once again, I don't have an alibi for this morning. I called into the office, telling them I was taking the rest of the week off. Then I took a walk to clear my head."

"Did anyone see you on your walk?"

Kendra shook her head. "No. I went around the lake and was thinking how lovely it was that I was the only person out there. When I left, I saw a woman walking a dog, but she didn't see me. Even if she had, I don't think Ramsay would find that much of an alibi." She sighed. "What a mess. And I can't help but feel like I helped contribute to Mona's death."

"In what way?"

"By having that stupid affair with Dillon to begin with. I don't know what I was thinking. We're both married. We *work* together. It wasn't my brightest moment." She folded some children's pants and placed them back into a box. "I think it went back again to the fact that I'm not feeling fulfilled at work. Or, actually, in my life. I've been stumbling around, trying to think of a way to add meaning and purpose. I just picked the completely wrong way to go about it."

Beatrice was still trying to piece together why Kendra thought she helped contribute to Mona's death. "Why do you think your affair contributed to Mona's murder?"

Kendra shrugged. "Because it certainly didn't help things. Plus, what if Dillon *is* responsible for Mona's death? As soon as he heard about Mona's murder, he was on the phone to me. He wanted to see if I could give him an alibi. The way he tried to sell it to me, it was to protect *both* of us, since he knew I didn't have a good alibi either. But I knew he was trying to save his own neck. He couldn't fool me. I wasn't going to lie to the police."

"So Dillon asked you to provide an alibi. Is that what's making you suspicious of Dillon. And why you're trying to piece together what happened to Mona?" asked Beatrice.

"That's right. I've started seriously wondering if Dillon might have blown up at Mona. Just momentarily lost control and lashed out at her." She shook her head. "Plus, Dillon has been acting out of character. I'm sure a lot of it is stress due to Mona's death. But he's been calling me on the phone all the time . . . just persistent. I'm not taking his calls now. He even tried to call me yesterday when I was at work."

"Wasn't he in the office, too?" asked Beatrice.

"No, he's taken the week off for bereavement leave." Kendra snorted. "It's deserted at the office now. Anyway, I have no desire to speak with Dillon. Any contact between the two of us at this point looks like collusion. Besides, I'd like to mend my relationship with my husband. Which isn't easy with Dillon calling me all the time. Now my husband thinks I'm being less than honest with him when I tell him Dillon's and my relationship is over."

"So you haven't spoken with Dillon at all lately? Not since he called to try to coordinate alibis?"

Kendra said, "I did take a call from him yesterday morning. I mainly picked up to tell him to stop calling me. It was getting ridiculous between him calling me at the office and then at home when I was around my husband. It was like you said—he sounded like he hadn't slept since Saturday. I wish I hadn't picked up the phone. It was amazing how quickly he'd changed his tune from telling me how in love he was with me to accusing me of a crime. Dillon immediately started blaming me for Mona's death. He was trying to twist it around somehow."

Beatrice frowned. "What was his reasoning behind that?"

"Dillon said I was ambitious and that if Mona let everyone know I'd had an affair with a coworker, it might mean that I wouldn't make partner at the firm. That I'd gotten rid of Mona before she could blab to the firm. I told Dillon he'd gotten it all wrong. Actually, I said he was deliberately misconstruing the situation *on purpose* because he was trying to throw me under the bus. That I seriously suspected that he might be involved in Mona's death. After all, Mona was driving him completely crazy. I'm sure that most of his current drinking problem was related to their relationship issues. In some ways, Dillon was sort of like me," she said wryly. "He was pinning all his hopes for a better life on us having an affair. Instead, what we both needed to do was evaluate our lives to see what was missing. What wasn't fulfilling in our lives and at work? But we leaped into an affair and managed to make our lives more complicated."

"What did he say when you mentioned you had your suspicions of him?" asked Beatrice.

Kendra sorted absently through the pile of clothes at her feet. "He wasn't very happy. In fact, Dillon kind of blew up. I told him his temper was one reason why I thought it was a likely possibility that he'd murdered Mona. I told him not to call me anymore. He sort of sneered at me that I thought I was so high and mighty, but he knew how I was. I said he didn't understand me at all. I wasn't merely ambitious—I was driven. And my drive isn't limited to the law firm. That's where he's going wrong. I'm driven to find a more rewarding life. I want to feel good about myself and what I'm doing." She sighed. "Mona's death made me realize that life is too short. And I don't even think Mona was happy. She never seemed satisfied. Which made me think that I needed to figure out for myself what was going to make *me* feel content. It's definitely not work. And it's sure not that affair."

"Do you think Dillon is going to keep pursuing you and trying to continue the affair?"

Kendra said tartly, "Good luck with that. It takes two to tango. But I got things wrong last time. I mean, Dillon would always say things about divorcing Mona, but I thought that was just him speaking out in frustration because they were arguing so much. Now, though, I believe I underestimated the depth of Dillon's feelings for me. He seems so frantic, the way he's trying to reach out to me. When he started blaming me for Mona's death, it was almost like he was trying to blackmail me into sticking with him. Maybe at this point, he's realizing how very alone he is."

Beatrice was quiet for a few moments. Then she said slowly, "Honestly, I have a tough time picturing the two of you together. I wouldn't have thought you and Dillon would have been in a relationship."

Kendra smiled at her. "I'm going to take that as a compliment, since Dillon seems so messed up right now. I'm not even sure I was all that attracted to him. He seemed at the time like a possible solution to my problems."

"I don't really know Dillon, so it's unfair of me to judge him from just the last week that we've been acquainted."

Kendra nodded. "He was a different person a few months ago. He was more light-hearted, funny. He seemed gentle. Then he changed, pretty abruptly."

"Any ideas why?"

"He started drinking too much," Kendra said immediately. "Dillon was always a social drinker, but we were aware that had changed. The partners said he was even drunk at the office. At first, they were saying he was coming back from lunch with alcohol on his breath. But then lately, they were whispering that he was intoxicated even when he arrived for work in the morning. There were other questions about him, too."

Beatrice wanted to hear what those questions were, but didn't want to appear too eager. She kept folding a stack of black tee-shirts, after sorting them by size.

Kendra continued slowly, "The firm's accountant talked with me about Dillon. She said that he seemed to be living larger than his income justified."

Beatrice raised her eyebrows. "That seems outside the scope of work, doesn't it? The fiscal irresponsibility of employees?"

"True. But I suspect the firm, especially the firm's accountant, was concerned about Dillon's income."

"Couldn't it have been income from Mona's boutique? Perhaps it was doing really well either online or in-person," said Beatrice.

"Maybe. But probably not to that extent." Kendra paused. "From the questions the accountant was asking, I wondered if they thought Dillon might be siphoning money from his clients."

"How is that even possible?" asked Beatrice. "Wouldn't that be something the firm would immediately be aware of? I'm sure that's the sort of thing an accountant would always be on the lookout for."

Kendra shrugged. "And it sounded like she was aware of an issue, but only recently. Dillon could have siphoned money that his clients received as settlement funds, reallocated them as attorney fees. Or he could have inflated expenses that he incurred while working for his clients, or his billable hours. At any rate, the accountant thinks something is fishy. Where there's smoke, there's usually fire."

"She noticed irregularities," said Beatrice in a quiet voice.

"Right." Kendra put a stack of clothing in one of the boxes. "And here's something else to consider. What if Mona started questioning where their money was coming from? From everything I've heard, Mona wasn't a stupid woman. Maybe Dillon told her he got a raise. But she'd have been able to see how big his checks were from the deposits in their account. Maybe Mona threatened to expose his secret."

"But that would mean an end to the large income stream for Mona, too."

Kendra said, "True, but from what I've heard, Mona was more upset about Dillon's affair than anything else. Maybe she was already planning on leaving Dillon, but wanted to make sure he got in trouble over the fraud." She sighed. "With Dillon's drinking and his life in total disarray, he was not really in any position to do an excellent job covering up the fraud, anyway. Maybe Mona was going to cooperate with the firm's accountant. Or even with the police."

Beatrice nodded. "Have you told Ramsay about this? Are the police involved, as far as you know?"

Kendra shook her head. "No. It's an internal issue for now. I don't think the firm would thank me for telling the police about the potential fraud. And who knows—maybe the firm has figured out a legitimate reason why Dillon would have the money he did. Maybe a wealthy relative died and left him money in her will." Kendra didn't sound convinced, though.

Kendra continued, "I know I'm a major suspect. The police are honed in on me. They realize Mona was threatening to tell everyone about the affair. They know the implications that would have for me at work—my office has a policy of no office romances. And they know I'm married. So the cops think I killed Mona to keep her from exposing the affair." She shook her head. "But I'm the kind of person who doesn't like to be controlled by anyone else. I told my husband last night about my affair with Dillon. I asked Paul to forgive me."

"How did he take it?"

"Not well," said Kendra. "But at least he's not a suspect. He was away at a conference when Mona was murdered." She gave Beatrice a rueful look. "Sorry. I've been talking your ear off about murder since we started. I'll change the subject. Discussing murder doesn't seem appropriate anyway, since we're in a church."

Kendra started chatting with great determination on other topics, focusing especially on Beatrice's involvement with the church and asking what a typical day for Wyatt looked like. Thirty minutes later, they were done with the sorting, folding, and boxing. Kendra headed for the parking lot, and Beatrice walked down the hall to Wyatt's office to see if he was free or in one of his many meetings for the day.

He was by himself and immediately looked up when she lightly tapped at his open door. "Everything okay?" he asked.

Beatrice nodded. "That was a very distracting activity. Good idea." She yawned. "I think I'm going to head back to the house and put my feet up for a while. Snuggling with Noo-noo is on the agenda, for sure."

He walked around his desk to give her a hug. "Okay. Can I drive you back?"

"No, no. I'm completely fine. I'll walk. Good luck with your afternoon. Lots of meetings?"

Wyatt brightened at the question. "Actually, no. The last meeting of the day got cancelled and the one before that got rescheduled. So I've got one short meeting in about an hour. At least, it's supposed to be short. We know how often that can change. How about if I leave here after that and we can hang out together at the house? I could pick up supper for us before coming home."

Beatrice patted her tummy wryly. "I can't even think about supper. We both got a big lunch in before everything happened. I'll have a snacky supper and a glass of wine after you get home."

Which was exactly what happened later. They both enjoyed a far more relaxing evening than they had at lunch. Wyatt had turned the "snacky supper" into a peaceful event by lighting candles and playing soft music. They ate a light meal of cheese and fruit, and Beatrice poured them both a glass of wine. It was cool enough outside to have the windows open and they could hear birdsong over the quiet music they were playing. Plus, they were able to watch the next episode of Grantchester that they'd taped. They sat on the sofa, a quilt over their legs and a corgi at their feet. Wyatt put his arm around Beatrice and she gave a sigh of contentment.

Chapter Fourteen

The next morning, Beatrice was up fairly early. With everything going on, she'd nearly forgotten about Tiggy and Dan's upcoming wedding. The plan was that all the Village Quilters would be coming up with decorations for the wedding and reception. Beatrice hadn't decided what she would contribute yet, and it was getting down to the wire.

"Everything okay?" asked Wyatt. He'd finished breakfast and had his laptop bag in hand, ready to head off to the church.

"Well, sort of," said Beatrice ruefully, a hint of self-deprecation coloring her tone. "I'm not fretting over what happened yesterday, which I know is what you're worried about. But I've realized I've neglected to brainstorm decorations for Tiggy and Dan's big day. That's going to be something I look at this morning. I'm starting to run out of time."

Wyatt smiled at her. "You still have time. And you always do a good job. Why don't you call Tiggy to see what she might want you to bring? You have some beautiful quilts and tablecloths, but you also have artwork."

"Good idea. You're right; she might be swamped with quilts by this point. Meadow's house is already pretty full of them.

Maybe she'd like to borrow some of the folk art I collected from my days at the museum."

Wyatt nodded. "So that's one thing you're working on today. What else is on the agenda?"

"Well, it's Wednesday, so I'm planning on being at the church tonight. Oh, I meant to tell you that Kendra Callan was sorting clothes with me yesterday. It sounds like she might be interested in the new member class."

"Great!" Wyatt said. He grinned at Beatrice. "Why do I have the feeling you might have been giving the church some free advertising?"

"Oh, I was definitely pitching the church," chuckled Beatrice. "Although I think Kendra was already sold. I didn't even realize she *wasn't* a member. She's regularly visited the church for a while. Anyway, she's not just interested in being a new member, she's also interested in church leadership."

Wyatt looked pleased. "That's fantastic. Great scouting, Beatrice."

"Maybe I'll see her at church again tonight. We'll see, anyway."

After Wyatt left, Beatrice's phone rang. It was Piper, looking to see if Beatrice could do a spot of babysitting for her.

Beatrice accepted with alacrity, quickly pulling the toy box she kept for Will out of the closet in preparation for his visit. Piper was there in minutes, holding a sleepy-looking Will. He gave Beatrice a sweet grin when he spotted her and held his arms out for her to hold him. She settled down with him on the sofa, and he rested his head on her.

Piper said, "Thanks for this. I've got to run a couple of errands that I've been putting off. I knew it would be easier to do them now, before the shops get too busy."

"No preschool today?" asked Beatrice.

Piper shook her head. "They're having a teacher in-service day for the preschool teachers."

Will, feeling more energetic when he spotted the toys, hopped off Beatrice's lap and headed over to the toy box to grab a story. Piper blew them both a kiss and slipped out the door.

Beatrice loved reading with Will. He was always so attentive. Plus, he'd memorized the stories and often chimed in excitedly while Beatrice was reading.

It wasn't long, though, before this idyll was interrupted by a rapid knock on the door. Beatrice grimaced. She had the feeling she knew exactly who was at her front door.

Sure enough, Miss Sissy was standing there, her emaciated form parked on her doorstep, arms akimbo. She glared at Beatrice. "Didn't tell me Will would be here."

"Miss Sissy, even *I* didn't know Will was going to be here. This was a spur-of-the-moment thing. Piper just needed to run some errands."

Miss Sissy only had eyes for Will, though, and wasn't interested in hearing Beatrice's excuses.

Beatrice noticed that there were a lot of cutting and grinding sounds emanating down the street. "Did you see any construction equipment or anything while you were outside?"

Miss Sissy narrowed her eyes at her. "No construction!" She stomped over to Will, who said, "Yayyy!" and reached out for her.

"Really? No construction? Because I'm hearing machinery."
She snarled, "*Deconstruction.*"

Beatrice blinked at the old woman. "Oh, right, right. You're having all that yard work done, aren't you? I somehow didn't realize the scope of the project. Chainsaws? Stump grinders? Wood chippers?"

Miss Sissy lost interest in their conversation, although she'd likely never actually gained interest in the first place.

"Actually, that reminds me," said Beatrice. "I need to do some yard work, too. Or at least continue the work that Wyatt started."

Miss Sissy was pointedly ignoring Beatrice now as Will took the old woman by the hand to show her the block tower he'd built.

"In fact, I got some pretty cool yard tools for a certain grandson of mine," continued Beatrice. She walked over to the closet again and this time pulled out a small wagon that held a plastic rake, hoe, spade, and watering can.

Will clapped his hands as Miss Sissy sullenly looked on. She clearly didn't want to work in Beatrice's yard. She hadn't even wanted to do yard work in her own yard, which was why there was a team of people working over there while she'd escaped down the street.

Will, naturally, immediately wanted to try out the new gardening tools. Beatrice grabbed her gloves and a hoe and headed outside, holding him by the hand. Miss Sissy trailed grouchily behind them.

There were actually some little areas that could stand to be raked after a storm had blown leaves from the trees the week before. Will happily, if ineffectively, attacked the leaves, raking them in various directions without actually creating a pile. Miss Sissy, cheering up a bit since Beatrice seemed not to be hovering around Will too much, helped him out by showing him how to work the rake a bit better. It was one of those endeavors where any gains were quickly decimated by the little boy joyfully jumping into the small piles. But they were outdoors, it was a glorious day, and Beatrice was making inroads on a stubborn patch of weeds.

Fifteen minutes into their tasks, they heard a bicycle bell and Georgia biked up to the yard, grinning at them.

"Will, aren't you such a big boy? You're helping your grandmama."

Will nodded solemnly. "Grandmama."

Miss Sissy said viciously, "I'm helping, too."

Georgia looked apologetic. "You're doing a very good job, Miss Sissy."

Miss Sissy and Will started their cycle of making progress and then immediately getting back to square one while Beatrice walked up to the road to speak with Georgia.

"How are things going on the wedding front?" asked Beatrice. "I'd get an update from Meadow, but she's so engrossed in the event that I'd never be able to stop her talking about it."

"Exactly! Meadow has truly taken things over."

Beatrice said, "In true Meadow fashion. But is Tiggy all right with that?"

"Absolutely. She's delighted that she hasn't had to deal with all the tiny details. All my aunt wants is Dan. The wedding is incidental."

"Are you running errands? I just realized it's a school day, isn't it?" Beatrice frowned. Sometimes, keeping track of the days of the week could be challenging when you were retired.

"It's a teacher Inservice day," said Georgia.

"Oh, same as for Will's preschool. I guess they try to do those on the same day. Hey, before I forget, how is the dress shopping going? That's the only thing I know of that was definitely on your plate."

Georgia said, "We found a dress! We did go to Lenoir, but Tiggy found the dress right away. When she tried it on, she burst into happy tears."

"An excellent way to know it's the perfect one," said Beatrice, smiling. "That's wonderful. I can't wait to see it."

"Why don't you come to the Patchwork Cottage? Tiggy's going to bring the dress over in fifteen minutes. It does need to be altered a little and Posy said she'd be happy to do it."

Beatrice said, "I'd love to come by. I'll bring Miss Sissy and Will with me."

Which was right when Piper drove up, waving at them all. "Mama!" said Will, dropping his plastic rake. Miss Sissy's expression was thunderous at having her playtime interrupted.

Piper parked the car and hopped out. She swung Will up into her arms, and he gave her a hug around the neck. "Big helper!" he told her earnestly.

"Oh, you've been a big helper?" Piper glanced over into the yard where his scattered yard tools and the little wagon lay. "Yard work? That's great, Will!"

Miss Sissy muttered something that sounded very much like *I've been a big helper, too.*

Beatrice said, "I was telling Georgia that I could take Will and Miss Sissy over to the Patchwork Cottage with me. Tiggy's bringing her dress over so that Posy can alter it."

"*The* dress, you mean?" Piper's eyes were big as she looked over to Georgia for confirmation. Georgia nodded. "Wow. So your shopping expedition was clearly a huge success. That's awesome!" She turned to Beatrice. "Thanks for offering, but Will actually has a playdate with his friend Henry. That's why I was scrambling to get my errands done before Henry came over to our house."

Beatrice was pleased Will was making friends, but couldn't help feeling a little sad that her grandson seemed to be growing up so very fast. It seemed like just the other day that he was born. "No problem," she said, reaching over to give Will a cuddle. "Hope you and Henry have a fun time playing."

"It looks like he had a fun time playing *here*," said Piper wryly, looking again at the scattered plastic yard equipment. "I haven't seen these toys before."

Beatrice smiled at her. "I saw them in the hardware store and couldn't resist them."

Miss Sissy started stomping off in the direction of the sounds of the chainsaws.

"Miss Sissy?" asked Georgia. "Want to see Tiggy's dress?"

Miss Sissy snarled in response and continued off home.

Georgia shrugged good-naturedly. "I guess Miss Sissy isn't so much a wedding dress person."

Piper bundled Will into the car, thanking Beatrice for looking after him. Georgia biked away, telling Beatrice she'd see her over at the shop shortly. Beatrice picked up the yard toys, put them back in the little wagon, let Noo-noo out to potty, and then headed inside to wash up before going to the Patchwork Cottage.

When she walked in, she saw Tiggy, looking radiant and wearing an A-line tea-length white dress with a high, lacy neck, and lacy full sleeves. "You look absolutely beautiful," said Beatrice, meaning it. She gave Tiggy a hug.

Tiggy was so excited that she had a hard time standing still. Posy, with pins in her mouth, waited a moment for Tiggy to settle down, which Tiggy finally did. She continued the careful job of hemming the dress.

"It's a pretty dress, isn't it?" asked Tiggy eagerly. "It's the prettiest dress I've ever owned. At first, I thought I'd be disappointed that I wasn't making my dress. You know—it's a special occasion, and I thought it might be more meaningful if I picked out and made every bit of the dress. But as soon as I saw this one when I was in Lenoir with Georgia, I knew it was the one." Tiggy beamed at Georgia, who was standing off to the side, giving her a grateful look.

The door opened, and the bell gave a vigorous clang at the vigorous push it was given. Meadow came in, eyes wide and grin wider.

"I spotted Beatrice's car in the parking lot and thought I'd stick my head in to see what was up. Plus, I have some book I'm supposed to be giving Beatrice. Look at you, Tiggy! You look like a princess in a fairytale," said Meadow warmly. "Give us a twirl!"

Posy said in as stern a tone as it was possible for sweet Posy to have that she thought the twirl should be postponed until after the pinning was finished.

A happy flush rose up Tiggy's cheeks. "I feel like a princess for sure, Meadow. It's a beautiful dress, isn't it?" It seemed Tiggy needed everyone to reassure her that the dress was perfect for the occasion, which they were all happy to do.

Meadow then launched into a monologue about the wedding reception food and how the pasta buffet was going to work while Tiggy smiled and nodded, still sneaking glances at herself in the full-length mirror Posy had set up.

Beatrice, at some point, managed to interject and ask both Tiggy and Meadow if they'd like her to contribute some of her folk-art collection for the reception. Tiggy eagerly accepted as Meadow started prattling off all the other decorative items that had been promised for the reception so far.

Beatrice, who'd heard quite enough wedding planning lately, slipped away for a few minutes to see what Posy had in the new arrivals section. Georgia gave her a wink as if knowing exactly what she was doing.

The recently arrived fabrics in a kaleidoscope of hues and patterns were sadly very tempting in their fetching fat quarter and charm pack bundles. However, Beatrice knew the last thing she needed right now was more fabric. Instead, she took pictures of the fabrics for inspiration later on, as well as pictures of the inspiration board that Posy had posted by the new arrivals, showing quilts that other quilters had created. Beatrice very nearly gave in to some rather innovative rulers and rotary cutters before quickly strolling over to the sitting area where Maisie the shop cat was sitting. The plump kitty gave a small mew in recognition as Beatrice headed toward her, then cuddled up against her on the small sofa, purring happily.

The bell on the door dinged again, this time more quietly as Thea Owen came in. Posy gave her a quick wave, pins still in hand, but the other women were too engaged in conversation to notice. Thea seemed to be wanting to speak with someone and moved aimlessly around the store before pausing in front of the new arrivals. She looked longingly at the fabrics before shaking her head. Then, spotting Beatrice in the sitting area, she walked slowly over.

"Hi there," she said a little shyly. "Beatrice, isn't it?"

Beatrice smiled at her. "That's right. How are things going, Thea?"

And, in response to that very innocent question, Thea immediately burst into tears.

Chapter Fifteen

B eatrice shouldn't have been surprised, she knew. After all, Meadow and she had seen Thea crying outside the grocery store when they'd spoken with her Monday morning. But somehow, the tears still managed to startle her. She stood up and gently led Thea to take her place on the sofa. Maisie, after blinking sleepily several times in confusion at the sobbing Thea, eventually snuggled up next to her, purring once again. Having the fluffy cat beside her seemed to calm Thea down. Beatrice handed Thea her tissue packet from her purse, making a mental note to replenish it again soon.

Meadow, of course, managed to approach them right then. She gasped, seeing Thea's red eyes and the tears the woman was unsuccessfully trying to swab from her face. She said, "Goodness gracious, Beatrice, what did you say to poor Thea?"

Beatrice said dryly, "I asked how she was doing."

"Can't you see she's not doing well at *all*?" scolded Meadow. She plonked herself down on the small sofa, which barely had enough room for Thea and Maisie. The shop cat gave Meadow a reproachful look before climbing into Thea's lap, where there was a bit more space.

After a few moments, Thea was able to speak. She said, "No, I'm not doing well at all. I've been so worried about what the police think about me. That's why I'm here in the shop."

Meadow frowned. "Why? To talk to the police? Or to hide from them?"

"Neither one," said Thea. "I wondered if you knew whether Ramsay and the other cops thought I killed Mona. And the other guy who died." She teared up again, but this time quietly instead of unleashing the storm that had poured forth moments before. "The police came back to talk to me, y'all. I keep thinking they're going to arrest me and put me in prison. It absolutely scares me to death. I just don't think I could stand it there."

Meadow said, "Of *course* you couldn't! And you won't have to, either. Ramsay believes no such thing."

Beatrice managed with difficulty not to roll her eyes. Meadow was fond of believing she and Ramsay were always on the same page, particularly when it came to people Meadow especially liked. Beatrice knew Ramsay, if he harbored dire suspicions about Thea, would keep them carefully to himself.

"Really?" asked Thea, looking hopefully at Meadow through teardrops on her lashes. "Did you ask him?"

"I didn't, but I don't have to. Nobody in their right minds could think you had anything to do with Mona's or Josh's deaths. Right, Beatrice?"

Beatrice gave what she hoped was a kind but noncommittal smile.

"I hope you're right," said Thea. "I haven't been able to sleep since Saturday. Now it's Wednesday. I feel like a total zombie." She shook her head. "I know Ramsay and the state police are having to weigh the fact that Mona thought I was stealing from the supply closet." She colored a little as she mumbled the words. "I didn't mean to do anything wrong. I wasn't even thinking about stealing. I looked at all that fabric that wasn't being used and something came over me."

Beatrice carefully kept quiet. The last time they'd heard from Thea, she'd claimed she hadn't taken anything from the closet. That she was looking in there and was planning to ask the guild if she could buy the fabric from them at a discount. But now it sounded as if Thea was confessing to taking fabric after all."

"Naturally something came over you when you saw the fabric!" said Meadow. "Something comes over me, too. I'm never happier than when I'm looking at Posy's new arrivals. It's such a happy time."

Thea seemed to be barely listening to her. "I was just so stupid. I should have known how it was going to look if someone saw me with those supplies. I feel so selfish, too. I know the fabric was meant for the entire group. I've also felt so ashamed of my behavior and ashamed of not having the money to do the things I want to do."

"What kinds of things are you wanting to do?" asked Beatrice curiously. "If you had more money?"

Thea gave a short laugh. "Well, eating what I'd like to eat, for one, without having to think about the price tag. But I'd also like to be able to relax by quilting. That's how I always used to wind down if I had trouble with insomnia. I mean, I like working at the grocery store. For the most part, anyway. People are usually pretty friendly and the work isn't hard. But they can't give me enough hours to make a decent living. I haven't been able to find another job, either."

Beatrice thought about Bibi, who was in the same boat as she looked to replace her job at the boutique after Mona fired her. Finding work in Dappled Hills was clearly not the easiest thing in the world.

"I'd also like to go back to school to get certified for something, but I don't have the money for community college," said Thea with a shrug. "So I feel like I'm kind of stuck."

"What would you be interested in taking at community college?" asked Meadow.

Thea said, "Well, when I've dreamed about it, I've thought about a couple of things." She hesitated and said shyly, "But the things aren't related to what I'm doing now at all. And they're totally unrelated to each other, too."

"Like?" prompted Meadow, leaning forward.

"I had a teacher one time who told me I caught on fast with the programming class I took." She shrugged again. "Maybe I could try that? I know they offer that kind of stuff at the college. And the other thing I thought about was early childhood education. I used to love babysitting when I was a teenager. I was the most popular babysitter around," she said with a laugh. She rubbed Maisie, looking sad again. The cat looked back up at her as if understanding how she was feeling. "But I know I can't afford the classes or anything, so it's sort of a pipe dream."

They were all quiet for a few moments before Meadow said, "Nope! I refuse to believe that community college is out of your reach. Beatrice, you know about things like that, don't you?"

Meadow fervently believed that Beatrice knew everything in the realms of academia and art. Beatrice cleared her throat. "It's not something I'm exactly an expert on, but you should make an appointment to speak with a financial aid counselor at the school. Sometimes they offer grants and scholarships, as well. Maybe the college even offers part-time work on the campus as part of a work-study program. You could even find out if Bub's does any sort of tuition reimbursement program."

Meadow beamed at Beatrice. "I knew you'd know of some workarounds."

Beatrice said, "You could also check to see if they offer some online or hybrid classes there. Those might be more cost-effective, if the college has them."

"Do you think I could do it? Be a student again?" asked Thea slowly.

"I think the first thing you need to do is to call up the community college and make an appointment to speak with them. Find out what all your options are," said Beatrice.

Thea nodded, smiling at her. Her smile faded. "But now I'm a suspect in a couple of murders," said Thea, winding herself up again. "I'll never have a new job, and I might even lose the one I've got."

Meadow's expression boded ill for Ramsay if he honed in on Thea as the murderer. "Now, now," she said seriously. "It won't help to fall apart. Everything is going to be fine. You'll keep your job. Things will start looking up. You've hit a bad patch, that's all. Everybody hits those."

Thea looked rather disbelieving at this. She hiccuped a few times then said, "Even you?"

Meadow snorted. "Of course, even me. I have to wrangle Ramsay, don't I? I love the man, but he can be a handful sometimes."

Beatrice was sure that what Meadow called a handful was likely Ramsay squirreling himself away to write poetry instead of pushing the mower around. Or Ramsay hurrying away from obsessive wedding prepping.

"Beatrice has bad patches, too," said Meadow, gesturing at her.

Beatrice nodded, although she wasn't at all sure her bad patches were in the same league as Thea's. In fact, many of her bad patches involved dealing with Meadow.

Meadow continued, "Did you even know Josh Copeland? It doesn't sound as if you were in the habit of eating out much."

"No, I didn't know him at all," Thea said quickly. "That's what I was telling the police. Why would anybody kill someone they didn't know?"

Beatrice noticed some movement behind Thea, and saw Edgenora, likely on her lunch break from the church office, walking past the shop's new arrivals. She gave Beatrice a small smile before studying the attractively displayed fabrics again.

"I can't win for losing," said Thea, shoulders slumped dejectedly. "I work as hard as I can, but I can never get ahead. Something happens and knocks my legs out from underneath me every time."

"What does that?" asked Meadow, ready to be outraged again. She seemed to be in the mood to take expressions very literally.

Beatrice said, "I think Thea means that as soon as she starts saving money, something happens. Like a car repair or something. Is that right?"

Thea nodded sadly. "I'm desperate to have a better life. When I was a kid, I never thought things could be like this. You know how when you're a kid and the whole world is like yours for the taking? You think you can be an astronaut or something. Then you start in with math and you find out you can't even add very well, so that dream goes out the window. I sure didn't think I was going to be scraping by like this."

She looked at Beatrice. "I've been heading over to church more, thinking that might help me get my head back in the right place. At first, I went to ask forgiveness for thinking about swiping stuff from the storage closet. The guilt has been driving me crazy. I used one of those free blood pressure monitors at the drugstore and my blood pressure was sky high."

"Quilting helps me with stress," said Meadow.

Thea nodded eagerly. "Me too. It's a great way to calm down. But I don't have the money for it."

A determined expression crossed Meadow's features. Beatrice had the feeling she knew what was coming.

Sure enough, Meadow said, "I tell you what you can do, Thea. I've been quilting for most of my life. You should see the stash I have. I've done my best to keep it organized, but the truth is that I have way too much fabric. You'd be doing me a huge favor if you came by the house and grabbed some of it. Otherwise, it's going to take over my house."

Thea's eyes grew wide. "Are you sure? You mean that?"

"You better believe it. Why don't you follow me back to my house and I'll show you what I have?"

Thea's eyes glistened again. "That would be amazing. Thanks."

Meadow said, "And again, don't you worry your head about being a suspect. I'm sure there are far better suspects in this case than you. I know last time you said Dillon and Kendra were looking to marry. That would sure be a lot easier with Mona out of the way."

Thea nodded and said slowly, "Maybe it's one of them. Maybe Kendra wanted Dillon all to herself and knew Mona wasn't going to give Dillon a divorce."

This seemed rather unlikely to Beatrice. Kendra was an independent woman who appeared to be eager to improve her marriage.

Thea's eyes grew large. "I forgot to tell you one thing. There's another reason I think Kendra could have done it. The police found my missing Mickey Mouse earring in the shop."

Beatrice and Meadow frowned. This clue seemed to point more to Thea than it did to Kendra. "You were in Mountain Chic?" asked Beatrice.

Thea looked abashed. She said, "Okay, the truth is that I went over there to talk to Mona, a few days before she was murdered. I wanted to ask her as a favor not to say anything about the storage closet—not to the police, or anybody. Anyway, while I was there, one of my earrings came out. Kendra *knew* those were my earrings."

Meadow knit her brows. "You're confusing me, Thea."

Thea tried to slow down. "Kendra saw me when I was finishing up my shift at the store before I went over to Mona's shop. She was trying to be nice to me and told me she loved my earrings. So Kendra knew they were mine. When my shift was over, I went to the shop to talk to Mona. Mona wouldn't even listen to me. Actually, she pretty much threw me out of the shop. When I got back home, I realized one of my earrings were gone."

"Do you know where you lost it?" Beatrice asked.

Thea shook her head. "It could have been on the sidewalk in between Bub's Grocery and the boutique. It could have been in the boutique, even. Do you see what I mean, though? Kendra could have spotted the earring, known it was mine, and pocketed it. Maybe she thought she was going to give it to me later. Or maybe she thought that she'd use the earring to set me up as a suspect after she murdered Mona. Either way, the police found the earring near Mona's body. And I had nothing to do with Mona dying."

Beatrice and Meadow were quiet, thinking it all through.

Thea continued, "I feel awful thinking like that about Kendra. She'd been so nice to tell me she liked my earrings. But Mona's shop was so clean, wouldn't she have found my earring if it had been in the shop for days? She'd just have thrown it in the garbage. That's why I think somebody took it on purpose to plant near her." Her thin shoulders slumped even more. "I'm starting to wonder if I need to start thinking about a move. Maybe I should go to Lenoir. There are lots more jobs there. Plus, nobody there thinks I'm a killer."

It sounded like a viable option to Beatrice. A way to escape gossip and seek better opportunities. But Meadow was horrified by the idea. She was always on team Dappled Hills, though.

"I won't hear any talk about that right now. You're tired and upset. We're going to head right over to my house and look at fabric."

Thea gave her a miserable look. "Are you sure Ramsay won't be upset about that? I didn't think cops were supposed to fraternize with the enemy or whatever."

Meadow's expression was fierce. "He better not be upset about that."

Meadow gave Thea a hand and pulled her up from the sofa. Maisie the shop cat gave Meadow an exasperated look, but then settled back down against a pillow. Beatrice stood, too, thinking she could speak to Tiggy for another minute and see how the pinning had gone.

Beatrice said, "You mentioned you had Ramsay's book for me, Meadow?"

Meadow snapped her fingers. "Right." She dug into her huge purse and thrust the book of poetry at Beatrice. "Your delivery from Ramsay. Some poetry." She made a face as if she'd eaten something that disagreed with her.

Beatrice took the book from her. "Actually, the poetry is supposed to be really good. I looked up the poet after I spoke with Ramsay. Billy Collins is a Poet Laureate."

Meadow seemed unimpressed by this information. "If Billy Collins can help me get ready for this wedding, then that's the only way I'll find him helpful right now." She looked around to make sure no one, especially Tiggy, could overhear her. But Tiggy and Posy were still getting the dress pinned. Thea, apparently having little interest in poetry, had shyly wandered over to watch while she waited for Meadow.

Beatrice said, "I thought everything was coming together well. The tasting menu goodies were great. We have a plan for the chapel's decorations, and Wyatt has nailed down the service. It'll be a group of good friends. I know it's all going to go smoothly."

Meadow still looked frazzled, but gave Beatrice a tight smile. "If you say so. I keep seeing these awful shows on TV and videos on the internet about weddings that go really, really wrong. Blizzards and such."

Beatrice quirked an eyebrow. "I'm pretty sure a June blizzard in Dappled Hills would indicate the apocalypse was upon us. In which case, a wedding is going to be the last thing on our minds. Don't you think you're getting too worked up about this? Tiggy and Dan certainly don't want you to make yourself ill over their wedding planning. The entire point was that everything was supposed to be simple, easy, and low-stress."

Meadow looked a little ashamed of herself. "I suppose you're right." But then she gave Beatrice a quick glare. "Although I do think you're starting to sound a lot like Ramsay right about now."

"Ramsay has the right idea. You're putting entirely too much energy into this event. You've always been the one I've looked up to as a person who knew how to relax."

Meadow gave a small smile. "I do usually know how to relax, don't I?"

"No one does it better! You're very laid back." Except when it came to protecting her quilting sisters. That was one area in which Meadow was always ready to do battle.

"Hmm. Food for thought," said Meadow.

"You haven't even made time to see your grandbaby lately," pointed out Beatrice. "That in itself is a very shocking development."

Meadow frowned. "Gracious. I hadn't even realized. It's been a while, hasn't it?" The look on Meadow's face indicated that she might run down to Piper's house, kidnap the little boy, and run off with him.

"You'll have plenty of time to catch up with him. In the meantime, put your feet up some of the time. Read a book." Beatrice waved the book of poetry in the air to emphasize the point.

"Well, I sure won't be reading that one," said Meadow dryly. "I do think I have a Nora Roberts book that I've been meaning to read, though." She reached out suddenly and pulled Beatrice in for a hug. Beatrice was startled enough to nearly lose her balance through the process.

"Thanks, Beatrice," said Meadow. "That's exactly the pep talk I needed. Onward!" she said.

"Onward to a nap!" said Beatrice.

"After I see about Thea," said Meadow. "Then I promise I'll consider a nap."

Chapter Sixteen

As Meadow and Thea were heading out, Bibi Norton was heading into the Patchwork Cottage. Thea gave Bibi a bemused smile and hurried out as Meadow babbled about her fabric stash.

Posy still looked busy with the dress pinning. It seemed there were quite a few alterations to be done. Bibi was glancing around the shop, looking a little lost. Beatrice, who knew the quilt shop as well as the back of her hand, said, "Looking for something?"

Bibi smiled at her. "A job. Do you know if Posy is hiring?"

Beatrice didn't think she was. At any rate, it should be easy enough for Posy to find help if she needed it. Apparently, there was a real glut in terms of available workers. "I'm not sure. Do you have a resume you can drop off?"

Now Bibi's smile widened. "Well, the jobs I've been applying for are in retail, and a resume isn't so much a helpful tool. I'll wait to speak to her. Looks like she's about up to her eyeballs right now in alterations."

Right at that moment, though, Posy apparently finished the process of marking the future changes. Tiggy walked off carefully to get changed, and Posy walked over to speak with the young woman. "Hi there! Can I help you?" she asked.

Bibi said, "Hi there. I was just wondering if you were hiring at all. I used to work for Mona at the boutique. I'm great with customer-facing jobs."

Posy's sweet face looked concerned. "Oh, dear. I wish I needed full-time help. I do have a girl helping me out, but I'm thinking she's not happy with the number of hours I can give her." She hesitated. Beatrice figured the whole process must be tough on Posy. She was the last person in the world who would want to reject anybody or make them feel bad. Posy said slowly, "Are you a quilter?"

For half a second, Beatrice saw a look in Bibi's eyes that made her think Bibi might be about to fabricate an answer to that question. She said, "No. But I love the craft. And I'm a fast learner—I can take notes, watch videos. I can learn enough so I can help direct your customers."

Posy looked down at her hands. "I see." She looked at Beatrice as if she wished she could give the onerous job of turning Bibi down to someone else. "I'm so sorry. I don't think that would work out well for my customers. Or, I suppose, for myself, either."

Bibi immediately said, "That's no problem at all. I totally understand. I hope you can find the help you're looking for soon."

Tiggy stuck her head out from the back of the shop to ask Posy a question about extricating herself from her wedding dress, and Posy hurried gratefully away.

"Another opportunity bites the dust," said Bibi wryly. She looked at Beatrice. "You're sure Piper doesn't need a babysitter?"

"I'm afraid she doesn't. Like we mentioned before, Meadow and I fight over Will as it is. If we had even less time with him, we'd be absolutely rabid." Beatrice gave her an apologetic look. "So no good leads on the job-hunting front, I guess?"

Bibi shook her head. "No. I've tried about everywhere, too. I'm thinking about living here and commuting over to Lenoir."

It was the second time in the last few minutes that Beatrice had heard someone talk about the possibilities inherent in the bigger town. "I suppose they do have more opportunities there."

"Well, they have a lot more retail, that's for sure. And they have lots of restaurants, too. I was thinking I could get a job as a waitress over there. The gas money won't be great, but if I work in a nice place, the tips will really help. Anyway, Dappled Hills has gotten a little scary lately, especially after another murder." She shakes her head. "It's gotten to the point that I'm keeping an eye on my back, even when I'm at the playground with one of the kids I babysit."

"Have the police spoken with you again about Josh Copeland?" asked Beatrice.

Bibi nodded. "No surprise there. I guessed they'd have to follow back up with everybody they spoke with the first time. But it was annoying how they approached me to ask me questions. I was walking through downtown, all dressed up for an interview, and one of the officers stopped me in the street to talk with me."

Beatrice winced. "Not very good timing."

"Nope. It's definitely not the best way to get a job, having the police quiz you in the middle of downtown. I had to tell them that I didn't have an alibi for Josh's death, since I live alone. All I was doing yesterday morning was getting ready for my day. I'm spending all my free time when I'm not babysitting trying to find a job and don't have time to go around killing people." Bibi paused. "I was hoping they could at least provide a little information about Josh's death. Or Mona's. Anything to make me feel a little safer here in town. But they were totally tight-lipped about everything."

Beatrice nodded. The police weren't going to be particularly forthcoming during a murder investigation.

Bibi said slowly, "Although I was able to *infer* some information. The cop I was talking with was asking a lot of questions about a quilter."

Beatrice frowned. "What quilter?" She hoped it was just Thea. Meadow would go ballistic for sure if there was yet another quilter implicated.

"Someone Mona knew. Someone she quilted with in her club. What's it called . . . a guild? Anyway, the police were talking about it so much, it made me wonder if it was a lead for the case." Bibi shrugged. "I want everything back to normal. And a job. Josh was actually one of the ones I hit up for a job, too. I guess I've knocked on about every door in town at this point. I told the cop the same thing, about asking Josh for work, I mean. Josh seemed like a nice enough guy. I think he wanted to help me out, but he didn't have an opening at the restaurant."

Beatrice said with a smile, "It's amazing you thought he was a nice guy, considering you'd have heard lots of propaganda from Mona attesting that he wasn't."

Bibi grinned at her. "Well, Mona was definitely biased. The two of them were honestly too much alike. Both of them cared just a little too passionately about their businesses. I mean, you have to have a life outside of work, you know? Those two didn't get it." She shrugged again. "And now they're both gone. I wonder what's going to happen to Josh's restaurant now."

"I've been wondering the same thing. Maybe Josh has some family to take it over."

Bibi brightened a little. "Maybe they'll need to hire again if it goes under new ownership. Plus, they might lose some of the staff they have right now. It would have been pretty upsetting for them to find Josh like that." She paused. "And new ownership wouldn't have heard Mona slandering me."

"Slandering you?" asked Beatrice.

Bibi nodded, looking down. "I wasn't exactly telling the truth when I said Mona fired me because I was asking for too much time off. She fired me because she thought I was stealing from the boutique." She snorted. "Can you believe it?"

"Stealing? Like the merchandise?"

Bibi said, "No. Like money. The thing was, Mona ran a very tidy, organized shop. But her bookkeeping was a disaster. If Mona ended up with less money than she thought she had, it's all because she didn't keep track of it. I would *never* jeopardize my job for petty cash. I know exactly how tough it is to get another one. And I liked that job, crazy as it sounds. Even with Mona being annoying, even with her yelling at her husband over the phone. I liked setting up the displays at the boutique and seeing the new clothes and accessories come in. I liked helping the customers find a special outfit."

Beatrice could see that a job at Mountain Chic would be something that would appeal to Bibi. She always dressed with pizazz and seemed to have a natural bent toward fashion.

"I didn't tell the cop about why Mona *actually* fired me, though. He'd have taken that and run with it, I'm sure. And I know I didn't kill her, so I'd be officially wasting his time. The police need to focus on finding *real* leads."

Beatrice asked, "Did the police ask you who you thought might have been responsible for the murders?"

"They sure did. I went back to Dillon again. I told that cop that I could totally imagine Dillon wanting to rid himself of Mona. It was unbelievable how she'd talk to him. I mean, *yell* at him, not talk. Mona acted like Dillon was completely worthless."

Beatrice frowned. "That's so odd that Mona had that attitude."

"Right? She had *no* respect for her husband. Maybe she started out feeling respect for him, and that feeling deteriorated through the years. From everything I'd heard, Dillon had put himself through law school, passed the bar exam, and had an awesome career. According to Mona, he was a total waste of space. Maybe Mona started thinking that way when she found out about the affair."

Beatrice asked delicately, "Did Mona ever express any concerns about Dillon's drinking?" She was thinking about what

Kendra had said—how Dillon had changed dramatically as he started drinking more.

Bibi snorted. "Concerns? Mona wasn't concerned about Dillon at all, from what I could see. She didn't like the way it looked for him to be drunk all the time. She was yelling at him for that, too, calling him slovenly or some such. Like I said to that cop, it had to be tough for Dillon to hear. Maybe it finally got to him, and he lost it. It might not have been something he planned on doing at all. He could have come by the shop to see her, she could have started in on him, and then he just reacted."

"Well, that certainly makes sense."

Bibi looked at her. "Do you think so? I hope so. I don't have anything against Dillon at all, but I'd like the attention taken off of me. I wasn't trying to throw him under the bus, but I wanted to make sure the police were totally aware of the situation between Dillon and Mona. I keep feeling like the police are questioning me because it would be convenient for them if I was the killer. They want to put someone behind bars for this, and as soon as possible. They don't care who it is; they just want to shut the case down."

Beatrice didn't say anything but thought that didn't sound like Ramsay at all. It was true that he was always motivated to bring the perpetrator to justice quickly. But that was because he wanted to restore Dappled Hills to the idyllic place it usually was. Plus, he wanted to get back to his reading and writing and do less policing. But Ramsay was always fair, cautious, and measured with everything he did.

Bibi looked at her watch. "I better head on out. I have more doors to knock on."

"More retail?"

Bibi shook her head. "I think I'm going to try my luck at some of the offices around here. See if anybody needs a receptionist. I'm handy on a computer, and I can answer the phone well." She squared her shoulders as if about to head off into battle again.

"Good luck," said Beatrice. "I know it's a tough thing to do."

"It is. But totally necessary. I'm fond of eating," she said, giving a rueful grin.

After Bibi left, Beatrice told everybody goodbye (giving the still-excited Tiggy a warm hug) and headed out herself. It was something of a relief to return to her little cottage nestled in the trees. Her head felt as if it were whirling with all the different bits of information she'd heard, and there was something about being home again that made a sense of calm come over her. Even better, she saw Wyatt's car and knew he was back early. On Wednesdays, sometimes he'd stay at the church without heading home first, if meetings ran late. When she walked inside, he was sitting on the gingham sofa with Noo-noo snuggled against him. Noo-noo gave her a doggy grin in greeting.

"How are things going for you today?" asked Beatrice, setting her purse down on a table. "I'm glad you made it home early."

He smiled at her. "It's going well. I know I have to get right back over to the church in an hour, but I thought I'd take a short break while I could."

"Felt the need to escape to some peace and quiet?"

Wyatt nodded. "Lots more meetings this afternoon. I figured if I could recharge my batteries here, then I'd be good for the rest of the evening."

"Do you want anything to eat? Or are you planning on eating at the church?" There was always a Wednesday night supper there, followed by various programs for both the youth and adults. The meal was usually things like chicken casserole, meaty pasta, tacos, sloppy joes, or various other easy to prepare and eat meals.

Wyatt said, "Oh, I'll eat there. But I may have a snack here. I didn't eat much lunch—I was too busy."

"The meetings?"

Wyatt said, "Well, that, yes. But also busy planning. The service for Mona is tomorrow."

Beatrice raised her eyebrows. "*Is* it? That seems very hasty."

"Dillon's idea. He called me first thing this morning and asked if he could come by the church and get the service hammered out."

Beatrice said, "Was the funeral home able to arrange it on such short notice?"

Wyatt said, "Unfortunately, Mona's body hasn't been released by the forensics team yet. Dillon told me that he needed some closure, though, so he asked for a basic memorial service at the church."

Beatrice thought that it was likely Dillon might not be looking for closure as much as a way to show that he'd cared about Mona. After Bibi's statement to the police regarding Dillon, he was probably looking for ways to make himself look like a devoted husband. Wyatt was always looking for the best in people, of course, which was what made him an excellent minister. Beatrice decided to keep her thoughts to herself.

She said, "Will Mona's family be able to make it here in time? I was under the impression that they lived out of town. At least, no one has mentioned that Mona had any in-town family."

"Apparently, Dillon called them, and they said they'd make it no matter what. He said they only lived a couple of hours away, so it wouldn't be too much of a drive." Wyatt paused. "Although I got the impression that Dillon wasn't very pleased that they were going to be in attendance."

"I can imagine that. Some of them probably blame him for what happened to Mona. Spouses are always prime suspects." Beatrice noticed Wyatt was looking tired. "Hey, why don't we get you that snack we were talking about? I'll put something together. How hungry are you?"

It turned out that Wyatt was fairly hungry, especially after the skimpy lunch and the brutal afternoon of meetings. Beatrice discovered that she was, too. Beatrice found a couple of frozen pizzas and decided she could treat them as a basic canvas. She dolled them up with fresh yellow and orange peppers, plump mushrooms, and a ripe tomato. In the end, enough food was consumed that neither of them was going to eat much at the church. Wyatt rallied with the food, and they had an animated chat about meetings and how some of them might be best managed via email instead of in-person.

They walked over together, when it was time, since it was a pleasant evening, a warm breeze gently blowing around them. As they walked into the church dining hall, which also doubled as a recreation center, they were greeted with a chorus of hellos.

Beatrice and Wyatt visited with everyone for a few minutes before heading over to the buffet to scope out the offerings. They decided dessert was going to be the only food they really had room for. Plus, who could resist? Someone had brought in double chocolate peppermint cookies which Beatrice made a beeline for. Wyatt picked up a slice of limoncello cake, which he said was basically like eating sunshine.

After polishing off the desserts, they went their separate ways—Wyatt to teach a class on unlikely Biblical heroes, including Job, Gideon, and Esther, and Beatrice to sit in on a class that was studying the story of Ruth. As Beatrice settled into a chair, she was pleased to see Kendra Callan in her class. Kendra gave her a small wave from across the classroom. It looked as if Kendra was definitely following through with her intention to spend more time at church.

An hour later, the class wrapped up and everybody set about talking. Beatrice quietly slipped out of the room, thinking she'd send Wyatt a text that she was heading home a little early. She did and then hurried out the church door . . . the minister's wife skipping out, she thought with a smile. But it had been a long day and Beatrice was starting to feel the effects of it. The only thing she wanted to do at this point was to take a warm bath and then curl up with a book and a corgi.

She heard her name being called out behind her and turned to see Kendra hurrying to catch up.

Chapter Seventeen

Beatrice smiled at her. "Hey there. It was good to see you in Bible study."

"I thought I'd come over and be part of the Wednesday night activities. Usually I can't make them during the week."

"What did you think?" asked Beatrice.

"Everybody was welcoming. The class was actually awesome. I didn't expect to hear as much history as I did."

Beatrice smiled. "Jim Bard is really into history and giving context to the Biblical stories."

"Well, I definitely enjoyed his take on things. And even the food was good."

"The church ladies know how to cook a good meal." Beatrice patted her stomach. "They may not be low in calories, but they're high in comfort."

"Comfort food is definitely what I'm looking for right now. I'm still stewing over these murders. Especially since I'm feeling like I'm in the bullseye as a suspect. Have you heard any updates at all on the case?"

Beatrice, of course, had spoken with Thea that very afternoon. Thea, who seemed to think Kendra was responsible for the murders and swiped her Mickey Mouse earring and planted it to implicate her. She didn't want to put Thea in any danger if Kendra *did* do those things. Nor herself.

Proceeding with caution, she said, "I know one of the quilters is worried about the police attention on her, too."

"I know how that feels," said Kendra wryly. "What's the quilter done? Why does she feel like she's a suspect?"

Beatrice said cagily, "She apparently lost something that was found near Mona's body in the shop."

Kendra frowned. "Okay. That's pretty vague. Was the quilter someone who shopped in the boutique regularly? She could have lost her item another time." She appeared to be approaching the issue as the lawyer she was.

"I don't think she was a regular shopper there, no." Thea, of course, didn't seem to have enough money to even buy an accessory at the fancy boutique. Beatrice hesitated. "She did mention having seen you near the shop at one point." This was a stretch. Thea had actually said she'd thought Kendra could have seen the earring on the sidewalk, realized it was Thea's, and pocketed it for later. But she was curious to see what Kendra would say.

Kendra immediately seemed wary. There was a defensive note in her voice as she said, "Well, I was often in Mona's shop. It's the best place in town to get professional clothing. I'm not saying I didn't feel a little awkward and conflicted shopping there, but it definitely saved me a trip to Lenoir. Or Charlotte, even. Besides, I like supporting local businesses." She paused. "Going back to the lost item. Did the quilter lose it the morning of Mona's murder?"

"Not the day of, but shortly before."

Kendra nodded. "I remember a nervous woman in the shop one day, who was asking to speak with Mona. I wondered what business she might have with Mona. I thought she might be about to ask her for a job, but she didn't look like she was dressed for an interview. She also didn't look like the sort of put-together person who would work in an upscale boutique."

"Did she speak with Mona?"

"No," said Kendra. "Mona wasn't there. I remember feeling relieved when I walked in and didn't see her. I always preferred dealing with the girl she had working there. Anyway, the woman was actually shaking. I remember chatting with her for a few minutes to calm her down."

Beatrice noticed that Kendra didn't say anything about the earrings. But she thought it was telling that the conversation had taken place inside the shop. Thea hadn't mentioned that. She'd gotten the impression that the episode had happened in the grocery store where Thea worked.

Kendra continued, "It doesn't look very good for the quilter, of course, as she told you. If she needs any representation, let me know. I can't rep her myself, naturally, but I could get someone else in the firm to do it." She glanced at her watch and said ruefully, "Here you were trying to get home early, and I held you up. Do you want a ride home?"

"Oh, I think I'm fine, thanks. Sometimes it's nice to stretch my legs a little. Glad you were able to make it to church tonight."

"See you soon," said Kendra. And she hopped into her car and drove away.

The next morning was busy at Beatrice and Wyatt's cottage. Wyatt was still pulling together the last-minute details for

Mona's memorial service. Beatrice walked Noo-noo, made them breakfast, and did some things around the house before they headed to the service.

On the way over to the church, Beatrice said, "Do you know if Mona's family was able to make it into town?"

"Dillon said they were to arrive last night." Wyatt sighed. "He also said they were very curt with him. He thinks they're blaming him for what happened to Mona."

"That might make things a bit awkward."

Wyatt said, "Hopefully everyone will be cordial. It's a tough situation all around."

Dillon had chosen the chapel for the service, thinking the turnout might be low. Mona didn't have a large family, Dillon apparently hadn't made a large group of friends in Dappled Hills, and neither of them were particularly outgoing. The chapel was decorated with red roses, which had been Mona's favorite flower. Wyatt told Beatrice on the way over that it was going to be a simple service with a soloist, a short Bible reading, and Wyatt giving the remarks. Wyatt had asked if Dillon wanted to speak, but had been turned down.

Wyatt checked on the audio equipment to make sure everything was working properly before the service started. He was tapping on the microphone at the lectern when Beatrice asked, "Do I need to run by the church office and pick up the programs for the service?"

Wyatt shook his head. "Dillon didn't think they would be necessary for such a brief service." But the expression on his face was a bit troubled. "I wish I'd had the chance to speak with Mona's family, just to confirm that the service was what they would want. Dillon didn't even provide their contact information to me."

"It sounds to me like Dillon didn't want them interfering with the plans."

Ten minutes later, a group of exhausted and emotional people entered the chapel and sat near the front. Not far behind them was Dillon, who wore a suit and tie, but who looked just as exhausted, or even more so, than when Beatrice had seen him earlier. Wyatt walked over to greet them and speak with them in low tones. They must be Mona's parents and brother. Beatrice noticed they didn't speak with Dillon, who was sitting across the aisle from them on the other side of the chapel. Dillon had his phone out and was carefully engrossed in the screen. He was just as careful not to look at Mona's family.

A few minutes later, some of the Cut-Ups walked in, Thea notably absent. But it was a Thursday near lunchtime and she could very well have been working. Posy came in and sat with Beatrice near the back of the room, giving her a little hug as she did. "I heard about you being at the restaurant when Josh was found," she whispered.

Beatrice nodded. "Wyatt was with me, which helped a lot. How are you doing? It must be hard to have lost two of your downtown neighbors like that."

Posy said sadly, "It really is. Hard and alarming at the same time. We had a meeting of the downtown businesses this morning. Ramsay was kind enough to attend. He reassured us that he and the state police were doing everything in their power to put an end to the violence. He's also assigned a very visible police presence to walk up and down the street."

"It's a pity it's come to that, but I think that's the smartest approach right now."

After a few more minutes to see if anyone else would file in, Wyatt started the service. Dillon seemed fidgety and, now that his phone was put away, couldn't seem to help himself from stealing glances across the aisle at Mona's family. Mona's family stared stonily ahead of them, refusing to engage.

"How very awkward," whispered Posy sadly. Beatrice agreed.

After Wyatt gave his remarks and the soloist had sung Psalm 23, Mona's family seemed to sense that the service was about to wrap up without anyone speaking. One member of the group stood up and walked to the front of the chapel. "May I say a few words?" he asked Wyatt.

Dillon stiffened, clearly unhappy that anyone was going to give a eulogy.

Wyatt smiled at the man and gestured to the lectern. He held a single page, clearly having decided on his speech in advance.

Now it was time for Dillon to look away. His gaze was focused downward as the man began to speak, as if he were fascinated by the polished base of the pew. He introduced himself as Brian, Mona's brother. It was one of those emotional eulogies, talking about Mona as she was growing up. Anecdotes about her fearless nature as a child and how she'd scare her parents to death by climbing trees and jumping out of them. How she had created a successful business through sweat and determination. Nothing was said about Mona's marriage to Dillon, which was a noticeable omission. Beatrice, from her spot at the back of the chapel saw some of the Cut-Ups looking at each other as if thinking the same thing. At the end, Brian said in a fiery tone that justice for his sister would be served. It sounded like both a threat and a promise. Dillon's shoulders were slumped, and he appeared to want to disappear into the wooden pew.

After Mona's brother sat, Wyatt delivered the benediction, and the service was over. There was to be no reception following. Considering what Beatrice had observed, she thought it was likely a smart idea to keep Dillon away from further proximity to Mona's family. Her parents and brother were now standing in a line at the front of the chapel, waiting for the gathered mourners to speak with them. Dillon hovered on the other side of the room. The Cut-Ups in attendance appeared to be taking the lead from Mona's family and didn't come over to talk to Dillon. In fact, no one was speaking with him.

Beatrice said to Posy, "I'm going over to stand with Dillon after we speak with Mona's family."

"That's very sweet of you. He'll appreciate it. The poor man looks like he wants to disappear. I'd join you, but I've got to get back to the shop."

They gave their condolences to Mona's parents and brother, then Posy hurried out. Beatrice stood next to Dillon, who looked very relieved to see her there.

"Thanks so much," he breathed. "I'm clearly something of a pariah. It's been very uncomfortable being here."

He looked more than uncomfortable; he looked positively ill. He was sweating and shivering at the same time. Plus, his gaze was unfocused enough that Beatrice wondered if he'd perhaps had something to drink before the service started.

"This is a nightmare," continued Dillon in a hoarse whisper. "I know the folks in attendance are going to talk about the fact Mona's family is treating me like a killer. Everyone in town is going to think I'm responsible for two deaths. Two! I didn't even *know* Josh Copeland." He hesitated, catching himself. "I mean, I didn't know him well. I know I spoke with him that afternoon with you and your daughter at the restaurant. But that's as much as I've ever talked to him. From what I saw, Josh seemed like a good guy."

Beatrice nodded. "You were looking pretty shaky that day. Josh was doing his best to get you feeling better."

Dillon gave a short laugh. "Good luck doing that. The only way I'm going to feel better is if the police arrest somebody. Somebody who isn't *me*." He gave a somewhat hysterical laugh, which earned him a few glares from Mona's family on the other side of the small chapel. He shook his head, noticing the looks. "I can't believe they think I could hurt Mona. I'm completely innocent. But they won't *talk* to me and let me explain."

"That must be very frustrating," said Beatrice.

"Incredibly. When I called to let them know the details for the service, they got off the phone with me as soon as they had the information. They never asked how I was doing at all. I would never have hurt Mona. This is all going downhill fast for me. I wouldn't be surprised if the law firm tries to force me out. They always worry about their image in town."

Beatrice raised her eyebrows. "That seems wrong. Lawyers, of all people, should know someone is innocent until proven guilty."

Dillon snorted. "Right. But appearances are everything to them. Just like they were to Mona."

"Were you able to give the police an alibi for Josh's death? I'm thinking if you had one, the police would likely think you couldn't have been responsible for Mona's murder."

Dillon said glumly, "No alibi. I wished I'd known I needed one. I was at home, trying to catch up on sleep. I haven't slept since last Saturday."

Wyatt left Mona's family and walked over. Dillon gave him a small smile. "How are you holding up?" asked Wyatt. His voice was concerned. Beatrice knew he was seeing exactly what she was. Dillon was a wreck.

Dillon shook his head. "I guess I'm not doing so well. I was telling Beatrice that I haven't been sleeping." He paused, watching as Mona's family collected their things from the pew and left the chapel. He sighed. "In some ways, I understand why they're acting that way. I think Mona had been telling her mom on the phone that things weren't great between us."

No one was in the chapel now. Wyatt gestured to one of the pews. "Do you want to have a seat? Talk about it a little?"

Chapter Eighteen

D illon hesitated. Beatrice wondered if part of him was more eager to head home and have another drink or two. But then he nodded, and they sat down next to him. It was a good idea on Wyatt's part. Dillon barely looked as if his legs would function too much longer.

Dillon looked down at his hands for a few moments, as if trying to figure out exactly what to say. He must have decided not to try to spin anything because he finally sighed and said, "I wasn't totally honest the last time I spoke to you, Beatrice."

"You weren't?"

He shook his head. "I said that I was trying to make my relationship with Mona work. But our relationship was totally beyond repair. I guess her family knows that, too. Maybe they also heard from Mona that I was having an affair." He looked at Wyatt. "I want to change. I really do. I feel so guilty about what happened. If I hadn't been cheating, if Mona and I had been a strong couple, maybe I'd have been hanging out with Mona in the shop last Saturday. She wouldn't have been murdered if I was standing there."

"Is that what you used to do?" asked Beatrice. "Hang out with Mona at the boutique?"

Dillon nodded. "That's right. I'd head over there and eat my breakfast with her at Mountain Chic before going to work. We'd talk about work, whatever was going on in the news, and life. It was sort of our time." He paused for a moment. "I don't know when things got so rotten between us. It didn't start out that way. Of course, it didn't help when Mona found out I was having an affair. She saw a text come in from the woman I was seeing when I'd walked away from my phone."

Wyatt asked quietly, "Is that when things started going downhill?"

"Yes. There were times I didn't feel like I could even stay in the same house with Mona. When she was hurt, she doubled-down on things. She wasn't even civil to me. Mona would follow me around the house and spew all this horrible stuff. I could tell she must really hate me."

"Had you started thinking about divorce?" asked Beatrice.

"I'd already started speaking to a divorce attorney from my office. I could tell our differences were irreconcilable. She and I were totally miserable when we were around each other. It's not a healthy way to live."

Wyatt asked, "Did Mona want the relationship to continue? Did the two of you consider counseling?"

Dillon shook his head. "Like I said, it had come to the point where I was sure Mona hated me. She was basically using me as a punching bag. At that point, divorce made the most sense. I couldn't handle being in the same house with Mona and hearing her yelling at me all the time." His expression was eager as if he needed to convince Beatrice and Wyatt. "That's what I was telling the police. I wanted a *divorce*. I had no intention of murdering Mona or anybody else. I never wanted anything bad to happen to Mona. In fact, I'd have been a lot happier if Mona ended up with a new lease on life and let go of her bitterness against me. I felt bad that she was so poisonous toward me. After all, I was the one who'd given her good reason to be that way."

Beatrice noticed Dillon hadn't answered Wyatt's question. She wondered if *Mona* had wanted the divorce. Maybe she'd wanted their relationship, as imperfect as it was, to continue. If she hadn't agreed to a divorce, what would that have meant for Dillon and his hopes to start a relationship with Kendra Callan? How desperate would Dillon have been to get out of that marriage?

Wyatt must have been able to read her mind. He said, "Did Mona agree to a divorce?"

Here Dillon looked down again. "She was coming around."

They were quiet for a few moments. Dillon gave a shaky sigh and looked again as if he might want to escape home for a drink.

Beatrice said, "Have you thought any more about who might have been responsible for Mona's death?"

Dillon rubbed his face. "Well, it sure wasn't Josh, was it? That's one person I thought might have done it. He and Mona were at each other's throats for a while there. Now I feel guilty that I thought Josh could be guilty." He gave a short laugh. "No wonder I can't sleep. I feel guilty for just about everything. But yeah, when the police talked to me, I was pointing the finger at Josh, mainly. Of course, Ramsay already knew about the problems between Mona and Josh. Those weren't really a secret, especially with both of them calling the cops all the time to complain about the other one. But now it's pretty clear that Josh had nothing to do with Mona's death. I guess I should have seen that it couldn't have escalated beyond petty stuff."

"What do you think happened to Josh?" asked Beatrice.

Dillon shrugged. "Well, his restaurant is right next door to Mona's shop. He probably saw something that made Josh dangerous to the killer. Maybe he was the kind of guy who thought he could blackmail the person. He seemed like the sort of overconfident person who might try something like that." He looked at Beatrice. "Do you remember me talking about a quilter who was upset with Mona?"

Beatrice nodded. Dillon said, "Did the police say whether they'd followed up on that at all? I know you're friends with Ramsay."

"I know the police have followed up with her," said Beatrice. "But they need evidence before they can arrest anybody, of course."

Dillon shrugged. "I thought there *was* evidence. The police asked me if Mona had a pair of Mickey Mouse earrings. I laughed hysterically when they asked me that. I couldn't imagine Mona wearing those. Maybe the earrings belonged to the person who killed Mona."

"Maybe so." Beatrice carefully didn't mention the connection between the earrings and Thea.

There was a noise behind them, and they turned to see Mona's brother entering the chapel. "Forgot something," he muttered brusquely. He reached down in the pew to pick up what looked like his mother's purse.

Dillon cleared his throat. "Hey, Charles. I'm sorry about Mona."

"Sorry about killing her, you mean?" Charles was clearly not in the mood to mend any fences.

Dillon turned even paler than he already was. "Charles, I didn't lay a finger on Mona. I would never do something like that."

"You can keep saying that. It doesn't mean I have to believe it." Charles's voice was curt. "Look, I know all about your relationship with Mona. She'd call up and tell the family all about it. How you were cheating on her. How you were drinking too much and making her life miserable. How you wanted to divorce her. I'm thinking you decided your life would be a lot easier without Mona in it. Is that what happened? Did you kill her because she wouldn't give you a divorce? Because she told me she didn't want to split up with you. Who knows why?"

Dillon said tightly, "I didn't do anything. She was going to agree to a divorce. We both knew our marriage had gotten to the point where there wasn't anything we could do to improve it."

Charles gave a harsh laugh. "Right. Well, maybe it was something else that made you kill her. Mona told our mom that she thought you were cooking the books at the law firm."

Dillon turned even paler than he already was. "That's a lie. Something she made up."

"Like I'm going to believe a single word that comes out of your mouth, Dillon. Listening to you is a waste of my time. I need to go comfort my parents. It's not easy losing a child, you know. Of course, you didn't think about the impact your actions were going to have on Mona's family, did you? Typical. You only ever think about yourself. Well, you're not getting away with this. One way or another, you'll get what's coming to you. Either the police are going to get evidence you're behind Mona's murder and fraud at your firm, or else you're going to drink yourself to death." He gave Dillon a dismissive look. "From what I can see, you're well on your way."

Charles strode out with his mom's purse as Dillon watched him go, looking even more devastated than he had before.

Wyatt said gently, "Is that true? Have you been drinking more than usual?"

Dillon silently nodded. He was quiet for a few moments, looking down at his shaking hands. "Before, I guess it was something I was doing to handle the end of my marriage. Or maybe just to deal with Mona and how she'd make me feel as soon as I came home every day. Then it became more of a habit—something I didn't even think about doing."

"And now?" asked Wyatt. "Does it feel like something you can control?"

Dillon shook his head. "No. Now it's how I'm dealing with getting through every day, especially since last Saturday. It's been more of an all-day problem lately, instead of an end-of-the-day problem. Plus, I used to feel like I functioned pretty well while I was drinking. I don't feel that way anymore."

Wyatt said, "There are some great resources locally. Our church hosts AA meetings quite a few days of the week. Would you like me to connect you with the group? Or give you their contact information?"

Dillon hesitated. He looked like part of him wanted to accept help and part of him wanted very much to continue on the same destructive path. He said, "Are the meetings on the church's online calendar?"

"They are. You don't have to let them know you're coming, of course. You just walk right in. From everything I've heard, it's a very welcoming, warm group of people."

Dillon nodded again. "Thanks." He stood up. "I think it's time for me to get back home now. Getting through the service while Mona's family were shooting me looks was exhausting. Maybe I'll be able to actually take a nap and get a little sleep this afternoon. Right now, I've got a lot I need to process, and the insomnia isn't helping."

Beatrice said, "Good luck, Dillon. The service went well."

He gave her a faint smile and headed out of the chapel. Beatrice and Wyatt looked at each other.

"That conversation was pretty draining, especially after everything that's gone on during the last week," said Wyatt. "Are you okay?"

"I'm doing a lot better than Dillon is doing, that's for sure. But you're right; that was exhausting. I hope Dillon connects with the help he needs."

Wyatt nodded. "There are great resources, but he's got to be willing to reach out." He looked over at Beatrice. "On a totally different note, what's the rest of your day look like? Any naps in your own future?"

Beatrice gave a wry chuckle. "Unfortunately, no. I'm about to meet up with some of the Village Quilters to get the chapel ready for Tiggy and Dan's wedding on Saturday."

Wyatt rubbed his face. "Oh wow. I'd totally forgotten that was this afternoon."

"Well, the memorial service wasn't supposed to be quite as tiring as it was," said Beatrice with a smile. "They're usually not exactly stressful things to attend. But this one was pretty tense."

"That's putting it mildly. Do you have enough time to run home and take a nap before everybody shows up?"

Beatrice shook her head. "There's not enough time for that. By the time I got home and got settled, it would be time to head back over." She shrugged. "I don't think it's going to take very long to prepare the chapel, honestly. Meadow has everything ready. The main thing is going to be removing the floral arrangements from the memorial service. Did Dillon not want to take the roses home with him?"

"No. He said we could use them in the sanctuary for Sunday's service and to take the rest to the retirement home so the residents could enjoy them."

"That's nice," said Beatrice.

Wyatt said, "Well, sorry you don't have a chance to rest up. If you need me, I'll be in my office." He hesitated. "Could I give the Village Quilters a hand?"

Beatrice smiled at him. "Thanks for offering, but we're in good shape. Besides, you've had a stressful time, yourself. Have some lunch and try to relax in your office for a little while."

The reminder about lunch made Wyatt frown. "That's right; you haven't eaten."

"I had a big breakfast. And Meadow is bringing sandwiches for everybody. We're going to eat in the courtyard before we start decorating the chapel."

Wyatt looked more cheerful at that. Meadow's sandwiches, like everything Meadow made, weren't the ordinary sandwich variety. "Okay. But the offer still stands. Let me know if I can lend a hand." He gave her a hug and walked out the door.

It was very quiet in the chapel. Beatrice sat back in the pew and took a deep, relaxing breath. Watching the sunlight stream through the stained-glass windows helped her blood pressure, which did feel elevated, start to lower again. The chapel bordered a courtyard, the one where the Village Quilters were going to enjoy Meadow's sandwiches, and she could hear the birds twittering at the feeders that volunteers filled. For the first time in nearly a week, she felt at peace.

Until she heard a loud voice coming in. Meadow, of course. She had Miss Sissy in tow. Posy had left her shop in the hands of her assistant again and joined the group. Beatrice helped carry several light boxes that Meadow and Posy were holding. Miss Sissy glared at Beatrice, possibly still annoyed by the fact her playdate with Will had ended so early.

Meadow looked around the chapel. "Say, what's all this? The roses weren't part of the plan. Did you get these, Beatrice?"

Beatrice shook her head. "No, we just had Mona's memorial service."

"*Did* you?" Meadow frowned. "I don't remember hearing about any memorial service."

Posy gave her an apologetic look. "Sorry I didn't let you know. One of the Cut-Ups told me about it at the shop. That's the only reason I knew."

"It was arranged very quickly," said Beatrice.

"Hmm." Meadow put her hands on her generous hips. "Almost as if Dillon didn't want anyone showing up." She paused. "*Did* anyone show up?"

Posy looked at Beatrice. She said, "Well, there would certainly have been more people there if they'd known about it. A few of the Cut-Ups were there. And a couple of downtown business owners came to pay their respects, as well as her family."

Meadow grunted. "Okay. Well, to each his own, I suppose. Although I can't imagine that's the sort of send-off Mona would have wanted for herself." She tilted her head as she looked at the roses. "The flowers are beautiful. But I'm not sure if Tiggy would want flowers from the memorial service of a stranger at her wedding ceremony."

"Wyatt said they were to go to the sanctuary and to the retirement home," said Beatrice. "In the meantime, we can move them to the church office. I can't remember what we're decorating the chapel with, not off the top of my head."

"Magnolia leaves and blossoms, right from my yard," said Meadow. "Simple, pretty, and free."

"The chapel will look beautiful," said Beatrice.

Meadow said, "It *already* looks beautiful. It's one of those spaces that doesn't need any sprucing up. But it will bring the outdoors in and really enhance the beauty of the chapel."

Miss Sissy growled, "Sandwiches."

"Right as always," said Meadow with a grin. "We have to keep our priorities straight. Let's have the sandwiches out in the courtyard. I might have brought a few other goodies along, too."

Chapter Nineteen

The courtyard always seemed like a haven to Beatrice. They walked through the arched, wrought-iron gate onto the cobblestones and over to a set of carved wooden benches that a woodworking church member had lovingly constructed. A couple of tall trees made a natural canopy to protect them from the sun. There was a fountain with dappled sunlight dancing on the water. The bubbling sounds made a nice background for their lunch.

"No Tiggy?" asked Beatrice.

"She had some errands to run, so she won't be joining us for lunch. But she'll be here before long to give us a hand with the decorating," said Meadow.

Miss Sissy was already opening one of the paper bags and reaching her skinny arm in to grab the contents. Beatrice intended to keep an eye on her own food. If she got too close to Miss Sissy, it might end up disappearing.

Posy carefully pulled out the contents of her bag. "Meadow, you've outdone yourself again."

Meadow beamed proudly at them. "I've been cooking up a storm, y'all. You know how it is once I get started in the kitchen. I just can't seem to stop."

Beatrice pulled out her food and saw a pulled pork sandwich made with two slices of fresh cornbread alongside. She peered inside the sandwich and her eyes opened wide. "Peaches and bacon?"

Meadow puffed up. "That's right! Sweet and tangy. And a dollop of coleslaw to add a little crunch and some coolness to counteract the heat."

In her head, Beatrice wasn't entirely sure how all the different tastes were going to come together. But when she took a tentative bite, she knew she shouldn't have doubted Meadow. It was, naturally, amazing.

Miss Sissy was already tearing through her food, which made Beatrice wonder if she actually enjoyed the tastes along the way. She wasn't about to ask her, though, and risk the old woman snarling at her.

Posy said, "Is this homemade pimento cheese in the little container?"

"Sure is!" said Meadow cheerfully. "With just a hint of heat in it with jalapeno. I thought it might be fun to dip some veggies in them."

Which, naturally, Meadow had thoughtfully provided. Roasted okra, orange and yellow peppers, and cherry tomatoes were packaged along with the vegetables. And the grand finale was a miniature pecan pie in every bag.

Miss Sissy wasn't the only one who finished eating quickly. Everyone appeared to be a lot hungrier than they'd seemed at the beginning of the meal. The more they ate the delicious food, the more famished they all seemed to be. At least, until they took the final bite of pecan pie.

"I'm stuffed," said Beatrice ruefully.

"Well, that's the entire point of the lunch," said Meadow, grinning at her. "It fulfilled its purpose."

"I'm just hoping I can stay awake while we decorate."

Meadow leaped up. "Good point, Beatrice! We should start moving. If we sit here and enjoy our full tummies and the beautiful courtyard any longer, we might end up nodding off."

They collected their trash, threw it away, and headed to the chapel to start the process of decorating. And, in the case of the flowers from the memorial service, *un*-decorating.

Miss Sissy was already getting the magnolia leaves out.

"Oh, Miss Sissy," said Meadow. "You're great to help, but I need to show you how we're going to arrange those on the ends of the pews."

Miss Sissy hissed at her. Meadow backed off. "Okay," she said.

Meadow murmured to Beatrice, "Miss Sissy is a handful today."

Beatrice nodded. "You'd think a scrumptious lunch would have made her more laid-back."

"I think it's all that yardwork taking place at her house. The change is making her grouchy, even though she *wanted* the change, to begin with."

Tiggy came into the chapel. She saw them there and burst into happy tears. "This is so wonderful. I can't believe I'm about to get married."

Meadow hurried over to give her a bear hug. "There, there! No need to cry, Tiggy."

"I know. I'm so happy, that's all." Tiggy pulled a folded handkerchief from the pocket of her sensible pants, dabbed her eyes and blew her nose heartily before putting the handkerchief away. "I can't think when I've ever been so happy."

Beatrice said, "Everything is coming together so nicely, Tiggy. It's all falling into place."

"How is Dan doing?" asked Meadow.

Tiggy said, "Oh, he's doing pretty well. He's worried about his procedure, of course. I've been thinking ahead about how to get him feeling better as soon as possible when he's recovering from the surgery. Healthy food is best for that, don't you think?"

Meadow wasn't much up on healthy food, being a Southern cook. She said, "Beatrice thinks so, I'm sure."

Beatrice said, "Wyatt and I have fallen off the healthy eating wagon lately. Wyatt was on a real kick not too long ago, though, and he'd slimmed down and was feeling energetic."

Tiggy nodded, looking excited. "That's exactly what I'm thinking. He'll have a lot more energy, energy that he can use during his recovery. I'll give him a lot of raw fruits and vegetables. Nothing processed. All whole foods. He'll be better in no time."

They chatted about the upcoming wedding preparations and about Tiggy's dress a little. "You looked lovely in the dress," said Beatrice.

Tiggy blushed. "Did you think so? I just love it. At first, I was going to make my dress, you know. But now I'm so glad I found this one. It's perfect. Georgia was a big help, taking me to

Lenoir. And it was a fun girls' trip. I'd tried looking for a dress, just briefly, by myself. I knew Georgia doesn't have a lot of free time, between teaching school and tending to her house and yard with Tony. I felt bad about taking up the tiny bit of free time she actually has. I went into that boutique to see if I could find a dress there and let Georgia off the hook. I didn't say anything to her about it, though, because I knew she wanted to have it be an activity we both did together."

Beatrice said slowly, "You went in the boutique? What day was that?"

"It was Saturday. I went there while y'all were all at the mixed media class. Georgia was occupied, and I could hop in there really quickly and see if there was anything that would work. If there was, we wouldn't have had to make the trip to Lenoir."

Meadow suddenly said, "Miss Sissy! Wow!"

They turned to see that Miss Sissy, with her gnarled hands, had been carefully putting together the arrangements for the ends of the pews with white tulle, blossoms, and magnolia leaves.

"I didn't know you knew anything about flower arranging," said Meadow in an almost accusatory tone. Clearly, Miss Sissy was doing fine without any instruction at all.

Miss Sissy ignored Meadow, continuing to construct the arrangements. Meadow hurried over to join her.

Beatrice said, "Tiggy, when you went into the boutique on Saturday, what did you see there?"

Tiggy snorted. "I saw a lot of really steep price tags. You wouldn't believe how much the clothes in there cost. And I didn't see anything that looked like a bride's dress. Maybe a couple that would have worked for bridesmaids, but that's about it."

"Who was working there?" asked Beatrice. In the background, she could hear Meadow trying to give Miss Sissy tips and Miss Sissy's scathing snarls in response.

"Let's see." Tiggy considered the question carefully. "There was a nice woman helping me. She was excited about me being a bride . . . her face lit up right away. She showed me a dress that came closest to a bride's dress, but it still wasn't right."

Beatrice couldn't picture Mona being the nice woman Tiggy was talking about. "What did the woman look like?"

Tiggy said, "She was young, well-dressed, pretty. She knew a lot about clothes. It wasn't her fault that the merchandise didn't work out for this particular bride."

It was clearly Bibi that Tiggy had spoken with. But Bibi was supposed to have been fired by then. What was she doing in the shop the morning Mona died?

Chapter Twenty

"You're sure it was Saturday morning?" asked Beatrice.

"Positive. I planned it that way so that Georgia would be tied up and wouldn't know I'd checked in there behind her back."

Beatrice had no desire to upset this emotional bride again. She hesitated, then said slowly, "Did you hear that the owner of that shop died?"

Tiggy's eyes opened wide. "Did she? No, I didn't know that. I did hear about a murder, of course. Actually, a couple of them. But I've been so busy with the wedding planning, Dan's health, and with getting ready to move in with Dan after the wedding that I haven't had time to read the newspaper or even think about what happened. How awful! That poor young woman."

Beatrice said, "The young woman who helped you is fine, actually—she was an employee there. It was the owner who was murdered." Bibi was a former employee then, technically, but there was no point in clarifying this for Tiggy.

Meadow called Tiggy over to okay the arrangements, which Tiggy did with more happy tears. Beatrice said, "I'm going to move the roses to the office." She took one arrangement in each hand and headed out of the chapel, her mind spinning with what she'd heard. Bibi had been at the shop on Saturday? She certainly hadn't mentioned that fact to anyone. It didn't mean she had murdered Mona, but maybe *she* had been the one who'd discovered Mona's body. Then, perhaps afraid she'd be a suspect, she might have left before anyone else came in.

Unless she *did* murder Mona.

Edgenora greeted her when she walked into the office. "Hi there. How are things going with the decorating?"

Beatrice gave her a distracted smile. She was going to need to call Ramsay as soon as possible, but for now she needed to focus on what she was doing. "Well, apparently, Miss Sissy is a whiz at flower arranging, which is something no one was aware of. So that's actually going really well. How are things going here?"

Edgenora said, "Well, there was a young woman in here a few minutes ago to see if the church was hiring."

"Was her name Bibi?" asked Beatrice slowly.

"That's right. She's tried to find a job here before, but this time she specifically asked if the church needed someone to help me out in the office. She said she was good at social media as well as with basic office tasks. I told her there weren't any openings for now." Edgenora shrugged. "In the future, if I want to cut back my hours, then maybe then. But right now, I'm happy with the way things are."

Beatrice nodded, frowning. "And she left?"

"I presume so. Her business here was over, after all."

"Got it. Okay, well, I've got a couple more arrangements to move here. They're designated for the sanctuary and the retirement home, just FYI."

Beatrice headed out of the office toward the chapel. She nearly ran into Bibi, who was carrying two laptops. Bibi gave her a tight smile. "Sorry," she said.

Bibi started walking swiftly toward the exit.

Beatrice stuck her head back in the office. "There's no reason Bibi should have a couple of laptops with her, is there? She didn't come into the building with laptops?"

Edgenora frowned. "No. I'll call the police."

Beatrice hesitated. "Maybe I can persuade her to bring them back in. Then we won't have to get the police involved." But then she started thinking about the fact Bibi had helped Tiggy at the boutique the morning Mona died . . . even though Bibi had been fired then. Maybe getting Ramsay involved sooner rather than later would be better. "Actually, let's call them. Ramsay can sort things out."

She hurried out of the church, Edgenora calling after her, thinking if she called Bibi by name that the church could at least recover the laptops. Maybe Tiggy was wrong about who helped her or what day it was, even though she'd seemed so positive. Maybe Bibi had gone to the shop to pick up her final check and then left before Mona died. If Bibi was arrested for stealing from the church, it was going to be a mistake that could impact the rest of her life.

Bibi was already in her car, and her face hardened as she spotted Beatrice. She must have seen from the way Beatrice had rushed out of the church, looking around her that she'd been found out. Beatrice moved in Bibi's direction, waving her down, trying to make her stop.

Bibi, perhaps thinking that Beatrice was heading toward her car, drove right toward her to stop her. Beatrice moved swiftly out of the way, but not before Bibi's car gave her a glancing blow. It was enough to knock her off her feet. She slammed her head on the curb. Beatrice could faintly hear the sound of Bibi gunning the motor and taking off from the church, as quickly as she could.

Chapter Twenty-One

The next few minutes were something of a blur. Meadow was there first, having been alerted by Edgenora. She was clucking at Beatrice. Edgenora called Ramsay to tell him that Bibi was no longer at the church and to look for her car elsewhere. Beatrice did manage, despite a pounding headache, to tell him what type of car Bibi had. The ambulance came to take Beatrice away, and Meadow insisted on climbing into the vehicle to accompany her there.

For Beatrice's part, all she wanted was to go to sleep. However, the EMTs were quite insistent that she not do so. They were putting pressure on her head, which was bleeding more than she'd realized.

Efficient Edgenora had also called Wyatt, who was doing pastoral hospital rounds. He met the ambulance at the emergency room entrance, his face pale and grim.

"I'm okay," said Beatrice in a steady voice, although she felt far less than perfect. If her head would stop pounding, it would certainly help.

The emergency room was thankfully, and unusually, very quiet, so Beatrice was taken back straight away. Once Meadow saw she was settled and with Wyatt, she had Tiggy pick her up and take her back to the church to finish her decorating. Beatrice was relieved. Meadow was a little much to handle when one wasn't feeling a hundred percent. And she had the feeling Meadow would grill the doctors and nurses, wanting VIP care for her wounded friend.

Soon she was all patched up. Right now, Beatrice mostly felt sore. The fall she took on the curb managed to not only knock her out, but to skin part of her face, head, and leg so that the wounds felt like a burn. It was likely that she might be quite a bit sorer later on in the day. Still, considering the circumstances, she'd come out of the situation extremely well—it could certainly have gone a lot worse. The doctor wanted to do a scan of her head just to make sure everything was all right, so there was a bit of waiting ahead of them before Beatrice could be discharged and head back home.

While they were in the ER waiting for the scan, Ramsay stuck his head around the door of the exam room. "Everything okay?" he asked gruffly.

Beatrice nodded. "It is on my end. But I'm more interested in whether things are okay on *your* end."

"Bibi is in custody. We'd have pulled her in for the stolen laptops alone, but she also confessed to the whole thing. Luckily, I'd read Bibi her rights before she did, so it's going to hold up in court. That's a good thing because we needed some more evidence against her. Her fingerprints did match a partial on the scarf used to murder Mona, but it could have been explained away because of her working there. Her confession is very helpful." He gave Beatrice a serious look. "Do you feel well enough to tell me what happened?"

Beatrice nodded. "I had a wicked headache, but that's subsided now with whatever drug the hospital gave me. Now I'm just sort of sore."

Ramsay took a seat next to Wyatt's chair and pulled out his notebook, ready to take notes.

"It all started very innocuously, I promise," said Beatrice wryly. "I wasn't trying to get killed today. I want to make that very clear."

Wyatt reached out to squeeze her hand. Ramsay said, "I'd never think you'd do something deliberately dangerous."

Beatrice nodded. "We were decorating the chapel for Tiggy and Dan's wedding, following Mona's memorial service. Tiggy came in and started talking about how everything was coming together. She mentioned that she was so relieved that she and Georgia had found a great dress in Lenoir. That she'd popped into Mona's boutique on Saturday to see if she could find something there before asking Georgia to take the time to drive her out of town."

Ramsay raised her eyebrows. "Tiggy was in the shop the day Mona died?"

"That's right. She'd timed it so that she was there when we were all at the Patchwork Cottage for the class Posy was hosting. I asked Tiggy who'd helped her, thinking it was Mona, before she'd been murdered. But Tiggy described Bibi."

Ramsay nodded. "Got it."

"Everybody was decorating the pews, and I needed to get the roses from the memorial service out of the chapel. After I put them in the church office, I was heading back to the chapel and spotted Bibi with a couple of laptops."

Wyatt shook his head sadly. "We probably need to look at locking up the classrooms when they're not in use."

Ramsay asked, "Did she see you then?"

"No. I wanted to make sure that Bibi wasn't supposed to have the laptops, so I checked with Edgenora. Bibi had been asking about whether the church office was hiring and hadn't come in with any laptops."

Ramsay said, "And you chased after her."

"Unfortunately. I thought maybe Tiggy had gotten it wrong somehow. I hoped to stop Bibi from making a big mistake by stealing from the church. Plus, I hoped I could recover the laptops. Those are too expensive to let them walk out the door. Bibi saw me rush out and look around, and I guess she put two-and-two together." Beatrice shrugged. "I'm not sure what her plan was, though. Was she just going to keep driving until she left Dappled Hills? Was it worth it for the two laptops?"

Ramsay said, "If it eases your mind at all, from what Bibi said, there wasn't any sort of major plan. She'd been acting on instinct—pretty poor instinct, if you ask me. All she could think about was getting away without being caught by the police."

"Did she admit to planting Thea's earring at the shop?" asked Beatrice.

Ramsay nodded. "She did. Meadow will be delighted to hear that Thea is totally in the clear. Bibi spotted the earring, scooped it up, and planted it by Mona's body to create a diversion." He sighed. "She did a good job with it. We were looking in another direction for a while. Apparently, when Thea lost the earring, Bibi absently pocketed it just to get it off the sidewalk at the front of the store. Mona was a stickler for keeping the storefront tidy."

Wyatt said, "Did Bibi say what made her do this?"

Beatrice knew that the motive was what tenderhearted Wyatt would find hardest to understand.

Ramsay looked at Beatrice. "Do you want to hazard a guess?"

"I think Bibi was feeling desperate. Also, Mona wasn't the easiest person in the world to spend time with. I'm guessing Bibi didn't plan on murdering Mona, but she snapped on Saturday. I've heard Mona was often condescending and could be snide. She was probably mostly snide to her husband, but I'm sure that could be extended to her employee, too. Bibi was having a tough time finding a job. I think she might have gone back to Mona on Saturday to ask to get her job back."

Ramsay snorted. "I'd imagine that would be a tough thing to do, considering Mona thought she was a thief. And it sure sounds as if she was right about that. You saw Bibi heading out of the church with a couple of laptops in her hand."

"Right. But in Bibi's mind, it was worth a shot. After all, Mona didn't know about any other instances of her thievery. Plus, Bibi said that Mona didn't do a good job with her bookkeeping. Maybe Bibi *was* stealing petty cash, but Mona might not have had proof of that. Mona could have just been going with her gut."

Wyatt said slowly, "So Bibi went into the shop to ask for her job back. Mona might have said something to upset her. And Bibi murdered her . . . on the spur of the moment."

"Right," said Ramsay. "That's basically what Bibi admitted to. She saw red, got frustrated, and lashed out. She didn't mean to kill Mona. It wouldn't be a good strategy for getting a new job, as we were saying. Then she remembered the earring that she'd placed near the register. She'd kept it in case one of their shoppers came in looking for it. But she realized she had a new use for it."

Wyatt said, "And what about poor Josh? I guess he must have seen something?"

Ramsay gestured to Beatrice again, and she gave him a wry look. "Well, Ramsay obviously knows for sure. I'm going to hazard a guess that Josh spotted Bibi leaving the boutique after Mona died. He'd have known who she was because she'd come into the restaurant asking him for work."

"Why didn't he tell the police?" asked Wyatt.

"I suppose he likely wanted to blackmail Bibi in some way. She doesn't seem like a very good target, considering she was running out of funds and looking for a job. Maybe he was just the kind of person who liked to exert control over others. To feel powerful." Beatrice shrugged.

Ramsay nodded. "Excellent deduction, Beatrice. That's pretty much what Bibi said. Josh knew that she'd been fired from Mountain Chic because she'd come asking for work. He realized she had no legitimate reason to be in the shop the day Mona died. He decided to blackmail her. As soon as Bibi did find a job, she would be spending a good deal of her income paying Josh off for keeping quiet. It was a future she didn't want to be part of. She met up with him early in the day. He thought she was going to pay him something from her meager babysitting earnings. Instead, she took him by surprise and killed him."

Ramsay stood up. "I should probably let you rest for a while, Beatrice. Sorry you got mixed up in the middle of this. Did they give you any idea when you're going to be discharged?"

"Soon. I'm going to get a scan, just to be on the safe side, then I'll be heading back home. And very glad to be out of the hospital." Beatrice made a face. The hospital was definitely not her favorite place to spend time.

"Good. I'm sure there's probably a good Billy Collins poem on illness or hospitals, but I can't think of it," said Ramsay thoughtfully.

"Maybe you should write one yourself," said Wyatt with a smile. "A Ramsay Downey original."

Ramsay put his notebook and pen away. "Not a bad idea, preacher. Maybe I'll finally have some time to do that with this case solved."

The scan, thankfully, showed nothing and soon Beatrice was discharged to head back home with Wyatt. He fixed them a quick supper, let Noo-noo out, and basically didn't allow Beatrice to do anything but relax. She'd relaxed so much that she thought she wouldn't be able to get a wink of sleep when it was time to turn in. But despite the disturbing day, she fell right into the arms of Morpheus and conked out straight away.

The following day, Friday, was a blissfully quiet one before the wedding on Saturday. Meadow did, of course, check in with her by phone.

"Ramsay didn't give me any information at all last night! I've been very worried about you, Beatrice, *very* worried."

Beatrice said, "But you knew I was fine when you left the hospital."

"Yes, but then Ramsay said something about you getting a scan for that nasty crack on your head that Bibi gave you."

Beatrice said calmly, "The scan showed everything was fine. Bibi's behind bars and the world is back to normal."

Meadow had a few wrathful words for Bibi in terms of how wicked she was to turn Dappled Hills upside-down to begin with. Meadow said, "Oh! Oh, I nearly forgot to tell you, Beatrice. I've got the most marvelous news!"

Beatrice sincerely hoped it wasn't related to the pasta buffet. In Meadow's search for wedding reception perfection, she feared that Meadow might do a last-minute ditching of the set plans for something more elaborate to honor the couple. She said warily, "I do hope you're still planning on doing the pasta buffet."

Meadow gave a hearty laugh. "Of course! Don't be silly. I wouldn't change something like that the very day before the wedding."

Beatrice reflected that it was precisely the sort of thing Meadow would do, *especially* if she were on a deadline. Meadow was so laid-back and so confident of skills (rightly so), that she believed she could take on anything.

"I hope no one else is getting married." Beatrice could imagine Ramsay running away from home if that were the case. Perhaps with a backpack full of poetry and serious fiction.

"No!" Meadow laughed again. "You're not usually so terrible at guessing. But then, you did just have a head injury." She paused. "Are you planning on covering that up for the wedding tomorrow? Or will you go looking like you've bravely made it through the wars?"

"I'll look more like a war victim," said Beatrice dryly. "But I might be able to exchange my bandage out for something smaller by tomorrow. We'll see how it goes."

Meadow said, "Got it. Anyway, what I wanted to tell you was that I spoke with Thea this morning."

"Already?" It seemed very early in the day.

"I needed to run to the store really quickly for some more parmesan cheese. You wouldn't believe how much grated parmesan you need for a pasta buffet. It's unbelievable. The point is, Thea was working the checkout line. Beatrice, she was just so relieved to have an arrest for the murders."

Beatrice said, "I can only imagine. She was so worried that she was going to lose her job at Bub's Grocery. And judging from the difficulty Bibi had in finding a job, it sounds as if Thea's worries were justified."

"Exactly. The store was nice and quiet and management wasn't lurking around, so she and I had a nice little chat before another shopper came up to the checkout line. It was actually quite annoying when the other shopper interrupted us. She was only buying an apple!"

"Weren't you only buying parmesan cheese?" asked Beatrice.

"Yes, but I wanted to speak with Thea. The other shopper could have gone through self-checkout. Interrupting our conversation, indeed!" huffed Meadow.

Beatrice felt a headache coming on. Whether that was a result of her head injury, her phone call with Meadow, or both, she wasn't sure.

Meadow finally found her way back to her original thread. "Before we were interrupted, Thea told me she'd spoken to someone at the admissions office at the community college. They've encouraged her to apply and are working with her for the tuition. Isn't that wonderful?"

Beatrice smiled to herself. "That's great news. She really reached out quickly, didn't she? We only spoke with her about it on Wednesday."

"And she called the college the very next day. She hasn't completely decided what she's going to focus on for her studies, but she has an appointment with her adviser on Monday. Isn't that amazing?"

Beatrice had to admit that it was honestly pretty amazing. "I'm glad. She should have a lot more options that way. And maybe she can find an area to work in where she really loves her job."

Happily, their conversation came to a quick end since Meadow had about a million things to do to get ready for the wedding the following day.

And the wedding ended up being a simple, lovely event. The chapel looked even more beautiful than usual with the magnolia and tulle on the pew ends. The weather cooperated in an amazing way—everyone said they hadn't seen a more perfect day. Tiggy was a shy bride, beaming with happiness, and Dan looked proud, if a bit uncomfortable in his new suit. Georgia was teary with emotion. Savannah was seemingly stoic until Beatrice spotted her impatiently swiping a stray tear away.

Meadow rushed from the chapel as soon as the service was over so she could get back home for last-minute preparations before anyone else. That was easy enough because the guests were busily taking photos on their phones of the couple and Savannah and Georgia to send to the happy couple later.

In the interim, Meadow lit the mason jar candles, made sure the food was warm, and set out the cold things. The Village Quilters, always a crafty lot, worked together to come up with all the simple but lovely decorations. Between the quilts and the folk-art Beatrice had brought over, the barn looked magical with the warmth from the candles and the quilts everywhere. Meadow's food was amazing, as always, and there was plenty of it for everyone, although Miss Sissy tried heartily to eat herself completely stuffed. From classic spaghetti to vegetarian lasagna and easy-to-eat ravioli, Meadow had it covered. June Bug had outdone herself with a magnificent cake. Although Beatrice had often thought many wedding cakes had a distinctive cardboard taste, June Bug's was a true culinary masterpiece. It stood tall and was adorned with delicate frosting.

Posy's husband Cork, who owned the local wine shop, had donated wine for the occasion. It flowed freely as heartfelt toasts were made to honor the happy couple.

Boris, always the canine wild card at events, was blissfully happy with a series of stuffed Kongs in the back bedroom. Ramsay checked in on him from time to time. Cammie, who was tiny and well-behaved, made an appearance wearing a white collar with white beaded faux carnations, which Georgia had made. She accepted the oohs and ahhs as her due.

But the best part of the evening was when there was an impromptu dance floor set up in the barn after Meadow pushed the kitchen table out of the way. Ash quickly came up with an appropriate playlist of music on his phone and attached it by Bluetooth to a speaker. The strains of old standards quickly filled the barn and, after Tiggy and Dan had shyly had their first dance, others joined in.

Beatrice smiled up at Wyatt, their arms around each other, remembering their own wedding as they swayed gently to the music.

About the Author

Elizabeth writes the Southern Quilting mysteries and Memphis Barbeque mysteries for Penguin Random House and the Myrtle Clover series for Midnight Ink and independently. She blogs at ElizabethSpannCraig.com/blog, named by Writer's Digest as one of the 101 Best Websites for Writers. Elizabeth makes her home in Matthews, North Carolina, with her husband. She's the mother of two.

Sign up for Elizabeth's free newsletter to stay updated on releases:

https://bit.ly/2xZUXqO

This and That

I love hearing from my readers. You can find me on Facebook as Elizabeth Spann Craig Author, on Twitter as elizabethscraig, on my website at elizabethspanncraig.com, and by email at elizabethspanncraig@gmail.com.

Thanks so much for reading my book...I appreciate it. If you enjoyed the story, would you please leave a short review on the site where you purchased it? Just a few words would be great. Not only do I feel encouraged reading them, but they also help other readers discover my books. Thank you!

Did you know my books are available in print and ebook formats? Most of the Myrtle Clover series is available in audio and some of the Southern Quilting mysteries are. Find the audiobooks here: https://elizabethspanncraig.com/audio/

Please follow me on BookBub for my reading recommendations and release notifications.

I'd also like to thank some folks who helped me put this book together. Thanks to my cover designer, Karri Klawiter, for her awesome covers. Thanks to my editor, Judy Beatty for her help. Thanks to beta readers Amanda Arrieta, Rebecca Wahr, Cassie Kelley, and Dan Harris for all of their helpful suggestions and careful reading. Thanks to my ARC readers for helping to spread the word. Thanks, as always, to my family and readers.

Other Works by Elizabeth

Myrtle Clover Series in Order (be sure to look for the
Myrtle series in audio, ebook, and print):

Pretty is as Pretty Dies
Progressive Dinner Deadly
A Dyeing Shame
A Body in the Backyard
Death at a Drop-In
A Body at Book Club
Death Pays a Visit
A Body at Bunco
Murder on Opening Night
Cruising for Murder
Cooking is Murder
A Body in the Trunk
Cleaning is Murder
Edit to Death
Hushed Up
A Body in the Attic
Murder on the Ballot
Death of a Suitor

A Dash of Murder

Death at a Diner

A Myrtle Clover Christmas

Murder at a Yard Sale

Doom and Bloom (late 2023)

Southern Quilting Mysteries in Order:

Quilt or Innocence

Knot What it Seams

Quilt Trip

Shear Trouble

Tying the Knot

Patch of Trouble

Fall to Pieces

Rest in Pieces

On Pins and Needles

Fit to be Tied

Embroidering the Truth

Knot a Clue

Quilt-Ridden

Needled to Death

A Notion to Murder

Crosspatch

Behind the Seams

Quilt Complex

The Village Library Mysteries in Order (Debuting 2019):

Checked Out

Overdue

Borrowed Time

Hush-Hush

Where There's a Will

Frictional Characters

Spine Tingling

A Novel Idea

End of Story

Memphis Barbeque Mysteries in Order (Written as Riley Adams):

Delicious and Suspicious

Finger Lickin' Dead

Hickory Smoked Homicide

Rubbed Out

And a standalone "cozy zombie" novel: Race to Refuge, written as Liz Craig

Made in the USA
Columbia, SC
08 February 2024

31705360R00117